Crave The Darkness

J. Anne Scott

TRIGGER WARNINGS

Blood / Gore

Detailed Violence

Talk of Sex Trafficking and Rape

Grief and Loss

Childhood Trauma

PTSD / Trauma Flashbacks

Religious Trauma Themes

Kinks List

Rough Sex

Sexual Physical Fighting

Biting

Spanking

Dom / Sub play

Praise

Degradation

Choking

Orgasm Denial / Withholding

PLAYLIST

"Darkness comes in many forms.
Heaven help the man that falls in love with mine."

J. Anne Scott

DEDICATION

Every woman has a little darkness in them. Some hide theirs away, while others let that Darkness out to play. Never be ashamed of your Darkness; own that shit!

PROLOGUE

Violet
Journal entry
Mother's Day 2019

MY MOTHER.

They say mothers are supposed to protect their children. Give them unconditional love and affection. Mothers are nurturing, caring humans, but mine wasn't. My mother wasn't really a mother. Sure, she gave birth to me, but she never was all the things a mother should be. I had a real mom for 5 years of my life and that's it. It's a shame I was too young to remember it. I remember some things but not enough for it to really count. My mother was horrible. She lied, hit, screamed, yelled, and put me down. There's a long list of things my mother did to me, and one day, I'll share them all. One day, maybe I'll write a book about my childhood when my mother passes.

Today, I'm only writing a brief version about her. Usually, you hear stories about abusive fathers and the things they have done. Kids who grew up without fathers. Well, I grew up without a mother. Although she was present in my life at times, she wasn't really. I used to be jealous of my friends who had such loving and caring mothers, and I wondered often why I never had that. Why didn't my mother love me the way those kids' moms did? What did I do wrong? Was I not meant to be loved?

My father loved me and always showed it. But it wasn't enough. There was something different about a mother's love that daughters needed. A bond that a father just couldn't give. My mother made me feel unwanted as a child, as a teen and as a young woman. I still feel that way even now. Her trauma has affected me all these years, even though I have cut ties with her now. Because of her, I find it hard to trust people, to believe someone when they say they love or care for me. A part of me still thinks I'm that child who is undeserving of love. Especially a man's.

CHAPTER 1

Right Place, Right Time

Violet, age 24
Toronto, Canada
May 14 2021

FUCK, I'M TIRED. Today was way more busy than it usually is on a Wednesday night; I think my feet might actually fall off halfway home. It's 11:30 p.m. and Little Italy Street is winding down for the night. There's only a few places left open later into the night, mostly bars and pizza shops. Besides that, though, this area of the city is dead. I love working in this part of the city. It really does give you a little glimpse into what Italy might actually be like. With its bistro tables outside the shops, cafes and Italian-themed restaurants, and wood oven pizza places. It lets us poor folks dream we are really in Italy for a day, and let's be honest, this is the closest I'm ever gonna get to traveling there, or any other country for that matter.

With a sigh, I let out all my frustrations from the day. I honestly do enjoy my job; working as a waitress at Ramano's isn't half bad. My boss is great, and since it's more of a family restaurant, there's no sleazy men trying to grab my ass, or ones I have to pretend to flirt with for some extra tips. God, I really hate men sometimes. The only downside is having to be on my feet all day, but I've worked worse jobs for less money, so I guess I shouldn't complain.

I walk past the restaurant toward the bus stop. The next bus doesn't come until 12:00. It's just my fucking luck I finish work one minute late for the 11:30 bus. I shake my head, annoyed, but at least I don't live far. If my feet weren't already dead from the night, I'd walk home. A few minutes from the bus stop, a horribly rusted black Honda Civic pulls up to the curb on the opposite side of the street, in front of Salotto Di Mezzanotte—a fancy, high-class bar. Whoever's driving that piece of shit clearly isn't going in there, so they must just be parking there to go somewhere else.

I'm not sure why, but I can't stop looking at the car as I walk past; my gut tells me it shouldn't be there. *Why do I give a shit where these assholes park?* I shake my head again and laugh under my breath. God, I really need to get home and go to bed. I pull my headphones from my pocket, untangling the cord that's jumbled up from being in there all day. Music always calms me down—something I got from my father. I'm surprised my first word as a kid wasn't some band's name, or that my dad didn't put me into music lessons when I was two, but I guess in a way, I should thank him for being so musically inclined. It just makes my taste in music better than most people my age.

Before I can pick a playlist to listen to, a car door loudly slams shut. The noise makes me jump, and I turn my head toward the black Civic I was eyeing before. Two men who appear not much older than me get out of the vehicle; they seem tense—fidgety, looking around. They're both wearing black jeans and black hoodies, the hoods pulled over their heads. It's hard to make out what they're saying to each other, but one keeps pointing in the direction of Giovanni's pizzeria. I turn my gaze toward the pizza shop, squinting a little. I've only ever been there once. It's rumored to be owned by someone in the Italian Mafia, used for money laundering and secret meetings, but people say that about many of the restaurants around here. It *is* called Little Italy, after all, so maybe it's true. All I know is their pizza sucks, so money laundering or not, I won't be going there again.

I steal another glance in their direction and catch sight of one of the men taking what looks like a gun out from behind his back. *No fucking way!* As quietly as I can, I run behind a brick wall of one of the shops, out of sight. My eyes must be playing tricks on me, or maybe I'm hallucinating from being so tired. There's no way that man pulled out a gun. Fuck, this is not good; my instincts were right. Hiding behind the wall, I peek my head out slightly to see what they're doing now. They're still arguing—maybe one of them has decided he doesn't wanna rob the place or kill them, whatever it is they're planning.

Dread coils in my stomach. I need to do something, but my head is screaming at me to mind my own business and get the fuck out of here. If this really is Mafia related, then that's their business. *But what if there's innocent people in there?* Fuck my stupid conscience, why can't I be one of those people who doesn't give a fuck about anyone but themselves? I unlock my cell phone and call Giovanni's. It rings a few times before someone finally picks up.

"Thank you for calling Giovanni's Pizza, what can I get for you?" the guy asks.

"Hi, I was just outside your shop, and there's some really sketchy men with a possible weapon outside. I think they might be trying to rob you, so you should maybe call the police," I warn him quietly.

"How many?" the guy asks flatly.

Okay... Weird.

"Um, just two," I tell him.

The man hangs up the phone on me so abruptly, it takes a second to realize he did. No "thank you," no nothing. Well, that's what I get for trying to be nice, I guess. Maybe he just wants to call the police as quickly as possible.

Attempting to be brave, I pop my head out again to sneak another glance, but as I do, my bus drives up to the stop, blocking my view. *Shit.* I need to get on that bus; I can't wait another hour for the next one. There's not much more I can do anyway, so I quickly come out from behind the wall and run to my bus as the driver opens the doors. After flashing my bus pass, I find the nearest empty seat by the window, so I can see the pizza shop. Once seated, we drive past the shop, and the last thing I see before we go too far is the two men walking into Giovanni's. I try to look back, but the shop is just a blurred silhouette. I hope whoever is in there can get out the back door in time. Or maybe I misjudged the whole thing, and the men could have worked there or owned it.

Stop worrying, Violet, it's not your problem, you have enough problems, I think to myself. When my dad turns on the news tomorrow, hopefully there's no story of a mass shooting at Giovanni's.

ALMOST HALF AN hour later, I'm finally home. I was so distracted by those men that I missed my stop and had to get off at the next one and walk my ass the rest of the way. Now, I'm even more tired and cold. I just want my bed and to forget this night even happened. After unlocking and opening the front door, I'm greeted by my dad passed out in his La-Z-boy as usual, beer cans littering the coffee table, and a sink full of dirty dishes. I roll my eyes, annoyed, and shut the door behind me. I'm too tired to clean up this mess; that will be tomorrow's problem. Maybe I'll get lucky and he'll be sober enough to clean it himself.

I kick off my shoes, the balls of my feet screaming at me to sit down and get off them. Once I'm in my bedroom, I shut the door and sit on my bed. I'm even too tired to wash off my makeup, so makeup wipes it is; my skin can be angry with me in the morning. Just as I'm about to lay down and get some much needed rest, my phone rings. *Who the fuck is calling me this late?* I turn my phone over to see an unknown number. *Fuck that, they can leave a message.* I decline the call and shut my eyes. My phone rings again, and I grunt, reluctantly answering it.

"Hello?" I say sleepily.

"Hello," says a man with a deep, Italian accent. "My name is Marco Berlusconi. I believe you called my pizza shop warning my cook about some men causing trouble."

Dammit! I should have known this whole thing would somehow backfire on me. It was stupid to think I could just anonymously call, and no one would reach out to me.

"Yes, I did. Look, if they didn't do anything wrong, or if they work for you, I'm sorry. I didn't call the police or tell anyone else. They just didn't look right, and I was worried, so I just called to let someone know, that's it," I tell him, hoping I haven't caused more bad than good.

"No need to apologize. I was just calling to thank you. Those men were looking to cause harm to my workers, and you saved them," he explains.

"Oh, well it was nothing really, I'm glad I was able to do something in time. I appreciate the call," I said, not knowing what to say to the man.

"I didn't just call to thank you; where I come from, when someone does something nice for someone else, or helps them in some way, we owe that person a favor. I am now indebted to you, so should you ever need anything, please call Giovanni's."

A favor? What the fuck is this guy talking about? If this man really is in the Mafia like the rumors say, then like hell am I taking a favor from him.

"That's okay, really, you don't owe me anything. I'm glad your shop's safe and have a good night," I say to him, trying to get off the phone.

"Buonanotte," he says in Italian as I hang up.

I stare at my phone; a man who may or may not be in the Mafia just called to thank me for saving his pizza shop from being robbed. As if my life didn't already have enough bizarre shit in it. I will *not* be calling that man for anything, no thank you. And, I will be avoiding Giovanni's at all costs. Placing my phone on my dresser, I close my eyes, trying not to think about today's events and hoping tomorrow will be a more simple day.

CHAPTER 2
First Kill

Violet

One week later

IT'S SATURDAY NIGHT, and my best friend Jenny is coming over for a girl's night. That means alcohol, snacks and talking shit about all the people we hate. Something we both enjoy doing a little too much—likely the reason we both don't really have any other friends. To be fair, I've always kept a small circle of friends since I was a child, preferring my own company to the kids I went to school with, but you can't blame me for that. A lot of them were dicks who spent more time making fun of me for who my parents were instead of getting to know me.

I was the poor girl whose parents were drunks and divorced. Not much was ever really said about my father, though; I like to think it was because boys at my school were afraid of him. Too afraid I would tell him what they said and he'd probably drive his car through their house. And they would be right. My dad is definitely not someone you want to fuck with. He spent most of his young adult years getting into bar fights and hanging out with my uncle's motorcycle gang. Even now, at fifty-five, he's still a tough ass.

My mother, however... The kids had no problem reminding me who she was. Most of the rumors were true. They loved to point out that she was a crazy bitch who would pick me up from school, drunk and wearing barely any clothes. Being the girl with the crazy parents stuck with me even after high school. It's been five years since I've spoken to or seen my mom. I cut her out of my life, and it was the best decision I've ever made. No good ever came from having her in my life.

Since then, it's just been me and my dad. I love him, but he makes it hard sometimes. As I finish that thought, old daddy dearest stumbles in through the front door, nearly taking it off its hinges with the force.

"Great," I say out loud, rolling my eyes at him.

Taking in his appearance, I'm all too familiar with how hammered he is. It's safe to say girls' night won't be happening—at least not at my house. I pick up the phone to call Jenny to see if we can move this party for two to her place. It shouldn't be a problem since we normally go to her place, but after her breakup with her douchebag boyfriend, Jack, she hasn't enjoyed hanging around her apartment much. It's as if his shitty presence still lingers, and it leaves her feeling a little unsettled sometimes. He was verbally abusive and treated her like shit. Although he never hit her, he did punch holes in the walls of their bedroom, and that was enough of a wake up call for her to kick him the fuck out; I'm so proud of her for doing it.

It's not easy ending things with someone who's abusive or a narcissist. I unfortunately know that all too well. I've had my fair share of bad relationships, but that's another story for a different time. Phone in hand, I walk back towards my bedroom, closing the door behind me, not even giving my father a second glance. I tap my finger on Jenny's contact, and the phone rings three times before she picks up.

"Hello?" she answers.

"Hey, girl," I sigh. "You mind if we hang out at your place tonight? You know who decided to stop at the bar on his way home from work and is now piss drunk. I have all the drinks and stuff, so I'll just bring them with me."

"Um, actually, I was just about to call you... I'm not really feeling well, would you mind if we did it another night?" she asks with a shaky breath.

"Oh my god, yeah, of course. Did you want me to bring you anything?" I ask, concerned. Jenny gets random migraines from time to time, so she must have had one come on.

"No, no! I'm okay, really, it's just my head, you know how it goes. Please don't come over, I'll be okay. I'm just going to lay down for a bit," she says, her voice sounding a little calmer now.

"Okay, yeah, sure. You rest up and call me if you need anything," I reply.

"I will, bye, girl!"

"Bye!"

I hang up the phone and toss it on my bed, letting out a breath of air. *Well great, guess I'll just stay locked in my room for the night.* A part of me says I should go to Jenny's and at least bring her some snacks, maybe some pain meds in case she's out. Even though she told me not to, knowing Jenny, she does need something but won't ask because she thinks it will inconvenience me somehow. *Fuck it, I'm going anyway, she can be upset with me later for trying to be a good friend.* I need to do something anyway, besides sit here all night and listen to my father who is now passed out in his chair and currently snoring his face off.

I quickly change my pants from comfy sweats to leggings and throw on a crewneck sweater. Once I'm dressed, I grab a bag from my closet to put the snacks in and head for the kitchen, passing by my unconscious dad. His favorite beer is in his hand and drool is trickling down his chin as he snores, not a care in the world. I shake my head at him, packing the snacks in the bag and writing him a quick note saying I'm going to Jenny's and I'll call him later. I stick the note on his case of beer, seeing as that will probably be the first place he looks once he wakes up.

Stepping into my black boots, I zip up the sides and head out the door. Jenny lives pretty close, so it should only take about twenty minutes to get to her place by bus. It's days like this that I wish I could afford a car, or have a dad who could drive me instead of one passed out drunk at 8:30 p.m. But alas, those are just not the cards I was dealt; the fates really fucked me over on that one.

I arrive at Jenny's stop three minutes later than expected—never can rely on the bus being on time, early or late. I walk up the street toward her place, passing by all the little bungalows in her neighborhood. Her neighborhood isn't ghetto, per se, but it's definitely close to it. The couple that live above her sure are. Whenever I've been to Jenny's, they are always on the porch smoking weed or drinking. Definitely not the classy type, but who am I to judge? Look where I come from; it's not much better.

When I reach her apartment, there's a car parked on the curb out front. It looks familiar, but I can't quite place it at first. Thinking it's probably someone for the people upstairs, I continue down Jenny's driveway, but an eerie sensation comes over me; the same one when those men tried to rob that Marco guy's pizza shop. I stop and look back at the car again. *Where do I know that car from?* My thoughts are interrupted by a scream coming from inside the house. I whip my head around to the side door.

Suddenly, realization sets in. I *do* know that fucking car—it's Jack's. *Motherfucker!* I run to the side door, grab the rusty doorknob and swing the door open. Frantically, I fly down the stairs. Never in my life could I have been prepared for the nightmare I stumble into.

Jack's back is to me as he straddles Jenny, sprawled out on the tiled basement floor, her legs trying to kick out beneath him. His hands are wrapped around her throat. Her face isn't visible from this angle, but from the way she's struggling, Jack is obviously choking the ever-loving shit out of her. He's trying to kill her. *Fuck! What the fuck do I do? How do I get him off her?* I can't push him off, because he's much stronger than I am, and I run the risk of him turning on me. I need to save her.

Panicking, I look wildly around the room for something I can use to hit him. On my left, there's a frying pan on the stove; I don't think, I just grab it and run toward Jack who is clearly too focused on killing Jenny to notice me coming up behind him. With a deep breath, I lift the frying pan above my head. Jenny's face is now visible over Jack's shoulder; her eyes are half closed, and she's quickly turning purple. The life slowly drains from her eyes as she fights to breathe, hands clawing at Jack's face and arms.

Anger blooms in my chest and I scream, swinging the frying pan down as hard as I can. It connects with Jack's skull, causing a deafening *crack* and spray of blood. His body slumps forward, landing on top of Jenny. I drop the frying pan and push him off her. Jenny gasps for air, clutching her throat, and I grab her, helping her sit up. She clings to me while coughing and sobbing in my arms.

"It's okay, I'm here, you're okay," I assure her quietly.

Her muffled sobs stop for a second as she tries to compose herself enough to speak. "He... He was going to kill me, Violet!"

"I know, but he didn't, okay? You're okay now."

I keep reassuring her that she's safe, that he didn't kill her, but she's clearly still in shock and doesn't recognize that yet. I lift her head off my shoulder and force her to look at me. Maybe if she sees my face, looks into my eyes, she will.

"Jenny, look at me," I tell her. She opens her tear-filled eyes, recognition forming on her face. "You're safe."

She nods in agreement, and slowly turns her head to look at Jack's body.

"Oh god, Violet," she says, placing a hand over her mouth, "what do we do? What if he wakes up... He'll kill us both!" She begins to hyperventilate and turns back toward me.

"No, he won't," I respond. "This is what's gonna happen. You're gonna go to my place and stay there, and wait for me to come back. I'll call the police and tell them what happened. He'll get charged, and you make sure to get a restraining order against him—and everything will be fine, okay?"

Jenny nods her head again. "Okay."

Jenny knows I've been through this with my parents. It was a daily routine at our house; my parents would drink, fight, and my dad would end up in jail for a few nights. My mom would get a restraining order so he couldn't come home—not for her own safety, but to keep me from seeing my father, to punish me for always taking his side.

I help Jenny up and grab her purse off the counter, placing it in her hands. "Go now, before he wakes up, and I'll call you once the police are here."

She hugs me one last time before she leaves. "Thank you, Violet. You saved my life."

She heads upstairs and once the door shuts, I finally release the breath I've been holding since I got here. Some of the tension leaves my body now that she's safe and away from here. I pull my phone from my pocket, ready to dial 911, when something shifts behind me. Looking over my shoulder, I gasp as Jack, now conscious, tries to pick himself up off the floor. Fear floods through me as I try desperately not to panic. *Shit.* I was really hoping he wouldn't wake up until the police got here.

"Ah fuck, you stupid bitch," he seethes, disoriented and sitting up slightly. He places a hand on his head, a large lump forming where I hit him. Squinting up at me, he looks over to where the frying pan is. "Did you hit me with a fucking frying pan? What the fuck?" he asks, clearly pissed at me.

The fact he has the audacity to be pissed off when he just tried to kill my friend—his ex-girlfriend!

"Yeah, I did, and I'll do a hell of a lot more if you ever try that shit again!" I yell. "And don't bother getting up. I'm calling the police to make sure you can never go near her again." I turn my back to do just that, but of course the asshole wasn't done with our conversation.

"Ha." He laughs. "You think the police will stop me? All you've done is dig her and yourself a bigger grave. She thought she could end things with me and I would let her walk away and live her life, after everything I've done for her!" he shouts.

I glare at him from over my shoulder. "You've done absolutely fucking nothing for her but cause her pain, and you're wrong; I'll make sure the police charge you and fuck you over!" I look toward the kitchen and take a few steps forward, away from him.

"You know, you came at the perfect time. I was going to fuck her once she passed out, teach her a lesson for thinking she could leave a man like me."

I stop dead in my tracks, his words making me freeze in place. Jack is fucked up, but his confession surprises me. I clench my hands into fists at my side, squeezing my phone so hard I could probably crack it. My heart is racing, and an unfamiliar feeling engulfs me—pure, undiluted rage. I place my phone in my back pocket and turn to face him. Jack's back is to me, one knee on the ground ready to get up. I walk toward him, but stop halfway and look at the frying pan. I bend down slightly and pick it up by the handle, its weight heavy in my hand.

Jack doesn't hear me come up behind him, and before he gets the chance to, I swing the pan in the air for the second time tonight and crack it over his skull, over and over again. Grunting and screaming after each hit. His body falls forward, but I don't stop. I can't make myself stop; images of my best friend laying helpless play over in my mind, and my vision blurs to red. Each blow to his head makes his skull and face cave in, but I don't look away. Blood coats my hands, my clothes, the tiled walls and even that doesn't make me stop. Even when the handle begins to burn my palm from the force of my grip.

It isn't until his lifeless body is still and silent, a growing pool of blood forming beneath him, that I finally drop the pan. Breathing heavily, I back away from him toward the wall, and I slide down it until I hit the cold tile. *Fuck.* Trying to control my breathing, my head rests against the wall as I look up at the ceiling. Once I'm a little more calm, I take stock of the room; there's so much blood—on the walls, the floor, the furniture, *me*. It looks like I bathed in it for fuck's sake.

The realization settles in; I can't believe I killed him. At least, I think he's dead. How could he not be? I force myself to look at Jack again. His face is so caved in, he's barely recognizable. *Holy fuck, Violet, what the hell did you do?!* I think to myself. I've never killed anything or anyone in my life. Unless we're counting a bug, but another human being? Fuck no! I stare at Jack's lifeless body. Regret doesn't surface, only anger and worry. Shouldn't I be sad? *What the hell is wrong with me?*

Deciding there's no time to dwell on my feelings—or lack thereof—I need to think of a plan. A way out of this, if there even is one. Jenny is safe at my place by now; she doesn't know what I've done. *What should I do? Think, Violet, think.* Do I start cleaning? Hide his body? Leave it here for the upstairs neighbors to find? No, I can't do that, they will blame Jenny for it, and I can't let her take the fall for this. Every possible scenario I come up with is utter shit. Clearly, watching all those late night crime documentaries didn't teach me anything—how to get away with murder, my ass! I'll just have to call the cops and say it was self defense; it's half true. And if they ask me why I felt the need to hit him so many times, I'll just say he didn't wanna stay down, that he kept trying to get back up and attack me. They'll believe that, right?

I sigh. Who am I kidding? They're never going to believe that. Even if Jenny explains to them that he tried to kill her, and I saved her, it doesn't excuse Jack with half his brains splattered on the floor. I look away in disgust and hope that by some miracle, something or someone will pop out of thin air and have the answer. Slowly, I scan the apartment and stop when an empty pizza box catches my attention, hanging out of the recycling bin near the stairs. Immediately, my mind goes to Marco and the night I saved his pizza shop from almost being robbed. *Nope, no way, not happening!*

There's no way in hell I'm calling a man who may or may not be—but most definitely is—in the Mafia . *You can just fuck right off, brain, because I'm not getting him involved.* Even though he did say he owed me a favor, and if I ever needed help with anything to call him. He *would* be the best man for this. I've watched enough Mafia movies to know they have guys for this; clean-up crews on their payroll, I guess you could say. People who can make messes like mine disappear, but what if he asks for another favor in return? *Am I going to live my life trading favors with the mob? Do I even have a choice at this point? Dammit!*

I pull my phone out of my back pocket and dial the number to Ronaldo's. It rings twice before someone answers.

"Giovanni's pizza," the man says.

I clear my throat. "Um, hi, this is Violet, Marco told me to call here if—"

"One moment." He cuts me off and the line disconnects.

"H-hello?"

Did he just hang up on me? Great. This is a mistake. I'm ready to throw my phone across the room when it rings, an unknown number flashing on the screen, just like that night.

"Hello? Is this Marco?"

"Hello, Violet," he answers. His voice is deep and raspy just like I remember it, with a hint of an Italian accent.

"I, um, I need to cash in that favor," I sigh. "I fucked up."

"Say no more, where are you?" he asks.

I tell him my location, and he says he and a few of his men are on their way, but until then, don't let anyone into the apartment and don't call anyone else. The line goes dead, and I sit and wait anxiously for his arrival.

About twenty minutes later, a text message from the same unknown number comes through. *'Here.'* I sit up and blow a deep breath out. *Well, here goes nothing, let's hope I don't end up* with *the same fate as old Jackie boy here.* I walk to the side door and cautiously open it. A very tall, and extremely handsome man greets me on the other side. He looks slightly intimidating and dangerous as fuck. Yup, definitely Marco. Two other men stand on either side of him, looking almost as intimidating as Marco, both with bulging muscles.

"Violet, I'm assuming?"

I nod, suddenly too stunned by his appearance and meeting him face to face. I had an image of what he may look like, but I wasn't picturing this. When you see men in the Mafia, in movies or in old photos, they are usually fat or bald. Not 6'3, muscular, and well... Hot. *Okay, Violet, let's not forget about the dead body on the kitchen floor.* Oh, right.

I clear my throat. "Come in," I say, opening the door more to let them in.

They walk one by one down the stairs, and once they're all inside, I shut the door and lock it then join them. I stop on the second last step, watching Marco as he gets closer to Jack's body. He crouches down beside him, examining his face—or what's left of it.

He whistles. "Is this your handy work?" he asks, turning his head toward me.

I swallow, trying to give some lubrication to my dry throat. "Yes," I reply, embarrassed by my actions for some reason. Is he thinking I'm some psycho girl with anger issues, or that I have the urge to kill people? "I-I've never done that before," I stammer, pointing to Jack's body.

Marco raises one eyebrow at me, confused. "Done what? Bludgeoned a man to death with a frying pan?"

"Yes, well, not just that, but I mean I've never killed anyone before in general."

Marco nods and stands, giving me a serious look. "I see. Well, my men will take care of the body, and while they are doing that, I need you to tell me what exactly happened here, and everything you know about the man you killed."

CHAPTER 3
The Awakening

Violet

I START FROM the beginning and tell Marco everything that happened, including some details about Jack, his family, and anything I can remember Jenny telling me about him. All the while, Marco's men are rolling Jack's body in black plastic tarps they brought in from their car. They all have gloves on and bits of Jack's skull have fallen out of the plastic. I just stare at them. Marco clears his throat, grabbing my attention back to him.

"Sorry," I say to him, shaking my head to try and clear my thoughts.

Marco looks at me, slightly concerned. "I imagine it must not be easy for you. If you prefer to wait in the car, I can have one of my men escort you; just because you killed a man doesn't mean you can't be traumatized by it."

"That's just it... I'm not traumatized by any of it—not the blood, his face, his death... Nothing," I admit to him. "I mean I should be, I've been trying to figure out why it was so easy for me to kill him." I don't know why I'm being so honest at this moment when I should be lying through my teeth.

Marco gives me a soft look, which is odd to see from a man like him. "That answer may be a bit more complicated, but I know what you are thinking, I can see it in your eyes, and no, you aren't a psychopath. You feel maybe a little too much, which is how you got into this mess. You saw a man not only hurting your friend, but a woman, and you sought your own version of justice for it."

I look over at the spot where Jack's body was only moments before, a smeared pool of blood the only thing left there now.

"That shouldn't matter. I should care, I took his life," I said, looking away from the spot and back to Marco.

"Would you kill your friend?" he asked.

I stare at Marco, baffled by his question. "No, of course not!"

Why the hell would he even ask me that? I love Jenny; I could never hurt her.

"What if you found out she was abusing children, or helping men traffic them?"

I look at him, dumbfounded. "I-I don't know, maybe, why are you asking me this?" I say, raising my voice a little.

"Because, you need to understand it's not the *person* that's easy to kill, it's what they have *done,*" he explains.

I let his words sink in, and the meaning behind them.

"Take me, for example; I kill men who steal from me, who threaten my family and my business, and who hurt innocent women and children who have no business being in our criminal world. I kill these men with no emotion whatsoever. In fact, I quite enjoy it sometimes, but that's beside the point. The point is, I lack emotion for those types of men, but not others, and people like us can use that to our advantage."

I squint my eyes at him, confused what he meant by that exactly.

"My men will finish things up here, we'll finish this conversation on our way to your place," he says.

He starts speaking to his men in Italian and gestures for me to follow him. I follow behind him up the stairs and out the door. I breathe in the fresh air, filling my lungs with it; the smell of blood and chemicals was making me lightheaded. Marco and I walk to a black Cadillac, and one of his men opens the doors for us. Marco moves to the side and lets me in first; who knew some men in the Mafia could be gentlemen? Especially a Mafia boss. We climb in, and Marco asks me my address then tells the driver.

It's slightly awkward being alone with him in such close proximity, but now that we're out of that crime scene and closer to one another, I take the time to study Marco—his olive skin, stern face and high cheekbones. He looks like an Italian model that could be in a JQ magazine for Mafia men. His age appears to be late thirties, with tattoos covering his knuckles, going up his arm. He's definitely covered head to toe in tats, and even though he's very attractive, he gives off an 'older brother' vibe, which is odd. I don't think I've ever felt that way toward an attractive man before, or any man for that matter. Even the men I date I don't feel safe with half the time, yet I'm sitting here next to a dangerous man who I barely know, and I'm perfectly at ease. This night just keeps getting stranger and more confusing on an emotional level.

We sit in silence, but I have questions I need answers to.

I clear my throat. "So, what happens when we get there? My dad's home, but he's probably still passed out drunk in his room."

Marco turns his attention from the window to me. "Does your father drink often?" he asks.

I pick at my nails, suddenly anxious. "Yeah, he's an alcoholic, has been since I was twelve."

Marco nods. "And your mother? Where is she?"

"I don't speak to my mother. She drinks as well, more than my father, and I haven't spoken to her in years; I would like to keep it that way," I say, wishing we could change the subject. My mother is the last person I need to think about right now.

"Fair enough, if she isn't involved in your life, then there's no reason we need to contact her. Is there anyone else you are close with besides Jenny and your father?" he asks.

"No, just them. I don't have much family. Most of them we've lost contact with, because they want nothing to do with my parents, and since I'm attached to them, they want nothing to do with me, either."

There's a hint of sadness in Marco's eyes, and I have to look away before I myself get too emotional. When I talk about my family these days, it doesn't bother me like it used to. I've accepted things, but still have my moments.

"I know how you feel. I don't have much family left either. Most have died; it's just me, my younger brother, Dante, and our mother, but in my world, I'm lucky to even have them—most don't," he says, his voice thick with emotion.

Figures I would relate more to a Mafia man's life than anyone else's.

"I've always wanted a brother, or any sibling, actually. At least then, I wouldn't have had to go through everything alone. I would have someone to protect me, and maybe I wouldn't get myself into so much trouble if I did." I laugh and Marco gives me a half smile.

"Maybe, although, between the two of us, my brother seems to get into the most trouble." We both laugh, some of my anxiety loosening its grip. "Violet, I would like to talk to you about possibly working for me."

"What? What do you mean, why would you want me to work for you?"

"Just hear me out. You have a skill, one that can be used for good. I know when you killed Jack, there's a part of you that enjoyed it, that made you feel relieved and at peace with him dead, so he couldn't hurt Jenny or any woman after her. Am I wrong?"

"No, I don't know. What does that have to do with working for you? You think just because I'm fucked, that I can kill a man and be fine? That makes you want to hire me to do what exactly? Become a hitman or hitwoman for you? Don't you have men to do your dirty work for you already? Why do you need me?" My anxiety is back in full force.

"I'm offering you a chance to help women. I'm not asking you to become my lackey, and yes, you are correct; I do have men for those types of jobs, but that's not what I'm asking you to do. I know this may be hard to believe, but my brother and I respect women dearly—most men in the criminal world don't. But there are a few of us that do. I'm sure you've heard of human trafficking?" he asks.

"Yes, of course, what woman hasn't?"

"Dante and I have been trying to crack down on the trafficking rings in Italy and New York, but these women, they don't trust us, and I don't blame them. They need a woman to save them, not a man. I've been wanting to open a shelter for women who have been abused or trafficked, so they have a safe place to start a new life. You could be that woman to help them, Violet. I have people who could train you to fight, to kill... Not that I think you will need much help in that department. You did kill a man with a frying pan, smashing his head into a fucking pancake. Think what you could do with real training."

"This is insane, what you're saying is insane—I can't work for the Mafia!" I stare at him, eyes wide, not quite believing what I'm hearing.

"Why not? You don't have much of a life here, Violet, so what's stopping you?"

"Um, how about the fact you're a criminal, and asking me to kill men for a living?!" *Is this really happening?*

"You're a criminal now, too, don't forget that."

Fuck, he's right. *Am I really considering his offer?*

"How would this even work? What would happen to my dad, to Jenny? Would I have to change my name and move to Italy? And what if I suck at it, or mess up? Are you gonna get one of your men to take me out?" I interrogate him.

His eyes narrow. "Seriously? You've watched too many Mafia movies. No, Violet, I would not hire someone to take you out if you mess up. We'll give it a year, and if you decide this is not the life for you, then you can pick a place you would like to live, with a new identity, and we'll go on with our lives as though we never met," he explains, as though this is a casual conversation.

"But what about Jenny? My dad, where do they fit into all of this?" I press.

"Your father and Jenny will go into witness protection of sorts. You can't visit them; you can only contact them using a burner phone, or a line we've made sure is secure. One thing about this life is that the ones you care for most are always at risk. You can't have friends, loved ones, no one that your enemies could use against you. Do you understand?" His tone is firm, and it's clear he means every word. I nod in a daze.

Marco continues, "You have no reason to trust me when I say this, but I promise you I will take care of your people as if they were my own. I may be a ruthless man—some may say the devil himself. But I keep my promises. If you agree to this, you need to agree to everything," he finishes.

I'm lost in thought when the car slows and stops in front of my apartment. I just about bolt from the car, wanting to see Jenny.

Marco places a hand on my shoulder, stopping me. "You go in first, see your friend. I'll give you a few minutes to explain things to her, then I'll come in. While you're in there, think about what I said."

"I will," I say quietly and open the car door, then run up to my dad's apartment. I forgot I'd given Jenny my keys. Checking to see if the door is locked, I turn the handle; luckily, she left it open. Likely too stressed to even realize she didn't lock the door behind her.

"Jenny!" I call out. My bedroom door opens, and she comes running out.

"Oh my god, Violet! Thank god you're back. I've been going stir crazy just sitting here waiting for you, not knowing what happened after I left. What *did* happen? Did Jack hurt you? Is he okay? I mean not that I really care—that bastard deserved to be hit with a frying pan—but did you call the police?" Jenny finally takes a breath.

"Jenny, I need you to calm down. I'll tell you what happened, just breathe," I say, hoping she'll relax.

She takes another deep breath. "Okay, I'm sorry. I'm just worried."

"There's nothing to worry about anymore. At least I don't think there is... I got someone to handle things and everything's going to be fine." I'm not sure if that last part is more for her benefit or mine.

"Wait, someone? You mean the police, right? You called the police after I left, didn't you?"

"Not exactly," I sigh. "Remember when I told you I witnessed an almost-robbery at Giovanni's, but I called the shop and stopped it from happening?"

"Yeah..."

"Well, I may have left a few details out about what really happened, but only because I was afraid something bad might happen if I told you too much. Long story short, the rumors we heard growing up about Giovanni's being owned by the Mafia... Well, it's true. It's owned by a man named Marco Berlusconi; he's the head of the Berlusconi Mafia crime family."

Jenny's jaw dropped. "What the actual fuck, Violet! Why the hell didn't you tell me this before? So the man who thanked you and offered you a favor that night was a mob boss?! Jesus Christ."

"I know it's crazy, and I'm sorry, I should have told you, but like I said, I didn't know if it was all going to bite me in the ass later if I told you when actually, it saved us."

"What do you mean, saved us? Is that... Is that who you called!?" she yells.

"Yes, listen, I know you're freaked out from Jack, but you need to trust me on this. I had no other choice but to call him, Jenny, I-I—" God, I can't believe I have to say these words to her. "I killed Jack."

Tears begin to well up in her eyes. "You... No, if this is a joke, Violet, it's not fun—"

I cut her off. "It's not a joke. I wish it was, I wish this whole night was just one big joke—but it's the truth. When you left, I was going to call the cops, but Jack woke up before I got the chance to. He said things, Jenny, about killing you, and making me watch… I just, I couldn't let him hurt you again. I lost it, and before I realized what I was doing, it was too late."

Jenny sobs, face buried in her hands. I look down at the floor, away from her sadness. I didn't expect telling her would be easy; she did love him at one point, and now, she's found out her best friend took his life away like it was nothing.

"The cops wouldn't have believed it was self defense, and they would have come after both of us. I couldn't let you go to jail for something I'd done—Marco was the only way out."

"I think I might pass out," she says, putting a hand on her head.

"Here, sit down." I sit next to her on the couch.

"You really did this? He's dead?"

"I'm sorry."

I'm not, but that's all I can think to say to her right now. I'm sorry I've hurt her, but I'm not sorry for killing him and protecting her.

She continues to sob next to me. "This is all my fault, you should have just let him kill me. Now you're involved with the Mafia, and a killer."

"Stop, don't say that! None of this is on you, and if I had to go back, I wouldn't change anything. Jack wanted you dead, and you would have expected me to just let him go ahead and do it? No, I made this mess, and I fixed it—it's over now."

"How can you be sure? What if the police find out Jack's missing? People might wonder where he is; how is Marco going to cover all this up?"

"Don't worry about that. Men like Marco have connections. They all do. He told me not to worry, and that he would take care of everything. Oddly enough, I trust the guy. I know that sounds crazy."

Jenny huffs and throws up her hands. "This whole night sounds fucking crazy, I feel like I'm in a fever dream, and I just want to wake up." She sniffles, wiping her tears.

"I know, me too."

There's a knock at the door.

Jenny stands up. "Shit, what if that's the police?!"

"No, it's probably just Marco."

She turns to me, frightened. "He's here? Violet, I'm scared, I don't want to meet him."

"It's fine, trust me. I wouldn't let him near you if I thought there was a chance he would hurt us. Come in!" I shout.

I grab Jenny's hand, giving it a little squeeze to help calm her nerves. Marco walks in, one of his men following behind him, guarding the door.

I introduce Marco to Jenny. "Jenny, this is Marco."

"Hi," she says meekly.

"Hello, Jenny. I would say it's nice to meet you, but under these circumstances, not so much. I understand you may be a bit worried, maybe even afraid of me, but I promise I mean you no harm. I'm here to help."

"Violet said the same. I appreciate you showing up and helping, but if you getting involved means Violet owes you something in return, then please leave," she says, her tone firm.

"Jenny—" I say, stopping her from saying something she shouldn't.

Marco cuts me off. "She owes me nothing. I owed Violet a favor, and now, her and I are even; Jack's body has been taken care of, and your apartment has been wiped clean. There's no trace of any evidence that you two were even there tonight, as if nothing happened, so I could walk away right now if I wanted to, but I don't—like I said, I'm here to help and make sure you are both taken care of.

"In order to make sure nothing traces back to you two regarding Jack's disappearance, I feel it's best if you disappear for a while. Nowhere crazy— maybe somewhere with family, a cottage perhaps." Marco has clearly done this before.

Jenny seems unconvinced. "Why do we need to disappear if you've handled everything? You said it yourself, there's no trace we were even there, so why do we still need to leave?"

"To ensure if anyone does try to contact you, you have a strong alibi. You can say you went on a road trip, that you were here all night packing," he suggests.

"What about Violet? Why are you only referring to me?"

"That's up to Violet. She can go with you. Use the same alibi. Or, she can come with me and start a new life."

Jenny stares at me, confused. "Violet. What the hell does he mean by that?"

"Marco has offered for me to come work for him."

"Violet, you can't be serious. You're going to join the fucking Mafia!?"

"No, it's not like that. I would be helping women like you."

"By killing!"

"I don't expect you to understand, Jenny. I don't even really understand it myself, but it would give me an opportunity to get out of this shithole and do something with my life, something good." I drop my gaze to the floor.

"Do you hear yourself right now? Something good—you'll be killing people." She shakes her head and turns away from me, like she can't bear to look at me.

"Bad people, Jenny. It's not the same thing as becoming a psychopath, killing random people."

She ignores me and turns her attention toward Marco. "Why her? Why do you want her?"

"Because I believe she has a skill for it," he says simply.

Her focus is back on me now. "You killed one man, and you think you can kill more? You know how fucked up that will make you?"

"I didn't cry when I killed Jack."

She blinks. "What?"

"I didn't feel anything when I killed him."

Jenny starts crying again. "Maybe you were just in shock."

I shake my head. "No, I wasn't. I felt nothing but relief when I did it. That's not normal, Jenny, but I saved you, and that's all that matters to me. Saving you is why I did it, and if I can do it again to save another woman, I would."

She's back to ignoring me and turns her attention to Marco once again. "How long do I go away for?"

"A few days, that's all. Nothing major," he says.

"And Violet? How long will she be working for you?"

Jenny avoids my gaze.

"You will disappear for a few days, but Violet will disappear for life. She can keep her first name but will need to take a new last one and leave her old life behind. No contact with anyone from her past—including you, unfortunately."

"Why?" Jenny whispers.

"It's too dangerous. It puts too many people she cares for at risk."

"Jenny, look at me," I say, pleading.

"I can't. How can I when I'm losing my best friend?"

"You aren't losing me, Jenny."

"Yes, I am." Her voice cracks on the last word.

"I'll find a way to get in contact with you and make it safe."

"No, I don't want you to. I feel like I don't even know you anymore, Violet."

"Jenny, I'm sorry about Jack—"

"Don't say his name, please." She closes her eyes and runs her hands through her hair. "I can go stay with my cousins. They live in Nova Scotia. It's a far drive, but..."

Marco interrupts her. "No need, I can have my men arrange a flight for you first thing."

"No, that's okay, I'd rather do it myself."

"I understand," he says.

Riddled with guilt, I say, "I can go back to your place with you tonight and help you pack."

"I'm not going back there."

"You can borrow some of my clothes then," I offer.

"No, thank you. I need to leave. This is all too much. If I'm leaving, I'm leaving today."

"One of my men can take you to the airport," Marco says.

"Thank you."

"Jenny, please wait!" Now the tears come.

"Goodbye, Violet."

"Bye, Jenny. I'm sorry."

I don't know what else to say. There's nothing I can say. I've hurt her too much. She can't even say goodbye to me properly. Marco tells the man by the door to escort her out and get the driver to take her to the airport and to pay. He also says to pay for the flight. She looks back at me one last time with tears in her eyes, and walks out the door. I cry for the first time today. Tears for a friend I no longer have.

"Would you like some time alone?" Marco asks.

"No, I'm fine." I try to pull myself together.

"I understand how hard that was for you. She will forgive you one day, when her judgment clears."

"I just wasn't expecting her to look at me like that."

"Like you are a monster?"

"Yeah," I mutter.

"You aren't, Violet, and one day, when more time has passed, she will see that."

"Yeah, maybe. So what now? Do I leave with you tonight?"

"No, you can have the night to get settled, pack, do what you must do, and I can arrange a car to get you in the morning."

"I still need to talk to my father," I say with a deep sigh.

"Yes, speaking of him; I'm surprised he's not out here yet. We weren't exactly being quiet."

"Oh, when he's drinking, the whole world could blow up, and he would still be snoring, sound asleep."

As if on cue, my father comes barging out of his room in nothing but his briefs. "Hi, honey, what's going on? Who's this?" he asks, slightly slurring his words.

"Dad, uh..."

Marco shows no sign that he's embarrassed or feels awkward about the fact that my dad has just walked out here in only his underwear.

"Dad, I need you to get dressed and sober up. We need to talk."

CHAPTER 4
La Famiglia

Violet Berlusconi
Present day, Lombardy, Italy

I DRIVE ALONG the smooth road to the Berlusconi mansion in my matte black Audi. I fucking love this car; only when I'm in Italy do I get to drive it. It stays at the mansion because Marco's got more security for that place than some military bases. Plus, it's more enjoyable driving it around the beautiful Italian scenery. I was never big on cars, considering I was too poor to even get my license, let alone afford a car, but spending years with Dante and Marco, I've developed a passion for them. Although Dante's more into his bikes, they both have their fair share of an extensive car collection; what rich men don't?

Marco called me this morning and asked if I could come home for a meeting. Home. It's funny, I've felt more at home with Dante and Marco then I ever did with any of my real family. That just goes to show you that home doesn't have to be a place, but can be people, too. Marco knew I was planning to come visit in a few days, but asked if I could come sooner. Next thing I knew, I was hopping on his private jet and heading home later that morning.

Usually, when Marco wants me home for a meeting, it involves family matters. Normally I would be a bit worried, but seeing as how I just spoke with Sabrina—Marco's wife—yesterday, and she didn't mention anything was wrong with her, Nikki—Dante's wife—or their daughter, I'm assuming this meeting is more on a business level.

I drive through the iron gates as they open, slowing down past the guards so they can see it's me. They wave me off and I speed past them, turning around the double driveway and park near one of the garages. The Berlusconi mansion always takes my breath away, with its old Italian architecture on the outside, and modern black marble on the inside.

Some days, I wish I could spend more time in Italy, but I'm needed in New York too often. It's been five years since I started my new life and officially became a Berlusconi. The first year, I needed to change my name and get a new identity; I asked Marco if I could take his family's name. As I grew close with him and Dante, they became like brothers to me, and they saw me as their sister, as well. It took some getting used to, having brothers and people who cared for me—it was strange.

I spent the first two years training to be a killing machine. I learned martial arts, self defense techniques, and took up knife throwing—which has been my number one method for killing. I enjoy the feel of a knife in my hand, the way the blade slices through a man's skin; it's much more satisfying than just shooting them and having it over with. I learned how to torture a man in many different ways with a knife.

My new 'career' started off helping Marco and his men on heists, infiltrating cartels and trafficking rings, and since then, I have started my own criminal organization—a helpline of sorts. A few women I have saved were hired on, giving them a purpose to help women like them. We have saved over 200 women so far. I've killed a lot of men since Jack. I lost count over the years, but if I had to guess, I would say at least 100.

Every now and then, I miss Jenny, and my father, too, but I don't regret losing them to protect them. They are both better off without me in their lives. My dad's doing pretty well, actually. Marco set him up in Costa Rica on a private villa, with guards and women; what man in his retirement age would complain about that? I haven't seen him since the night I showed up with Marco. We speak once a year on a burner phone to catch up. I've tried to do the same with Jenny, but she never answers, and that's okay. She's safe, and Marco still keeps tabs on her for me. She's married now and seems really happy, and that's all that matters.

I walk up the cobblestone steps but stop when I hear Dante's motorcycle. I turn to see him and his wife, Nikki, coming around the driveway. Dante kills the engine when he parks as I walk back down the steps. When I first met Dante, he was a major fuckboy; he had that whole playboy 'I only fuck and don't love' kinda attitude, and he has fucked almost every woman in Italy and half of New York. He did hit on me the first few weeks I was here, and I told him off each time, but now we rip into each other like siblings. Neither of us can ever take the other seriously.

We have had our moments where our relationship grew sour, especially when he was a dick to Nikki when they first met. I had a hard time with both him and Marco when they first met their wives, but those are stories for a different time. Let's just say their relationships had quite the rocky start. Who am I kidding; they were a fucking disaster, but they made it through.

They have both grown so much since then, and their love for Nikki and Sabrina can't be matched. If you told me when I first met Dante that he would become a father, I would have laughed. Get a girl pregnant, maybe, but a father who takes the role seriously? No. Now, though, I can't see him any other way. He's an amazing father to their daughter, Lily. As tough as he is, he has no problem doing the whole daddy-daughter tea party dates, and it's hilarious to walk in on him sitting in a little pink chair, with his blacked-out inked arms holding a little tea cup with his pinky up.

Dante gets off his bike, and takes off his helmet, as does Nikki. Her face looks a little flushed, but not from wearing the hot helmet. She seems a little embarrassed to see me standing here. *Huh, interesting.*

"Hey, Nikki," I say.

"Hey, Violet, I didn't know you were coming for a visit!" Her black hair fans out around her shoulders. "I would give you a hug, but I'm all sweaty from our ride." She gives me an awkward smile.

"All good. How was your ride?" I ask.

"Um, it was good, really good!" she says quickly, looking at Dante and blushing.

He smirks. "Yeah, we just went for a little joyride." He winks at her and she blushes even more, her face turning a bright shade of pink.

She turns her attention back to me. "I'll catch up with you later, Violet, I'm gonna go shower," she says, running past me and up the stairs.

"Okay!" I yell back to her. I smile at Dante, who is still smirking. "Joyride, huh?"

"Yup, just a joyride," he replies.

I look at his backpack resting on the seat, half unzipped with a black skull mask peeking out of it. He is so full of shit.

I look back at him and cock one eye brow. "Mhm."

His little joyrides he takes with Nikki are no secret to me. Men tend to forget that women love to talk, especially about sex, and even though Dante is like a brother, I never turn down a good sex story; it gives me good dirt on them if they ever try to annoy me.

"Hey, don't judge, just because you're practicing abstinence doesn't mean the rest of us happily married people are," Dante says, taking a dig at me.

"I'm not practicing abstinence, dickhead, you make me sound like a fucking nun. I just don't feel like wasting my time with men who dont know what the fuck they're doing."

That, and I have unfortunately been cursed with attachment issues when it comes to men. I can't just fuck a man and walk away, and seeing as how love is not in the cards for me, why bother putting myself through all that? Men can't be trusted, let alone with my heart. Been there, done that, and I'm not going through that pain again; I would rather kill one than date one.

Dante pulls me from my thoughts. "Speaking of nuns, Marco and I need to talk with you about something that needs to be taken care of—better yet, some*one*."

"I figured as much," I say, walking up the steps with him.

"He's in his office," he tells me as we head into the mansion.

"Where's Lily?" I ask.

Usually, she would be running to me by now. I love that little girl more than anything; I would die to protect her and the rest of this family. Children of my own isn't something I want, but being an aunt to Lily is by far the second best thing that has happened in my life.

"She's out in the garden picking flowers with Sabrina."

"Go see her, I need to shower before our meeting anyway," he says.

"No amount of soap can wash away those sins, Dante." I laugh at him. "But yes, please do."

Dante rolls his eyes at me and heads upstairs. I make my way to the back door to the garden, and little giggles come from Lily as I approach; I smile seeing Sabrina chase her around. Her curly brown hair bounces when she runs. It's hard to believe she's three already. Time keeps moving way too fast with her. Next thing you know, I'll be showing up to her high school with Dante threatening every boy. Knowing Dante, he will probably continue homeschooling her if he has his way.

Sabrina laughs as she chases Lily and finally catches her in an embrace. Sabrina and Nikki are polar opposites; they were best friends before they married the Berlusconi brothers, and are now sisters-in-law. When I first met them, I couldn't believe they were friends—Nikki is covered in tattoos, with black hair and navy highlights that give her an edgy look. Whereas Sabrina is more girly, with her honey-brown hair and brightly coloured clothes. But personality wise, Sabrina is more of a hardass, and Nikki is soft and sweet.

They may be polar opposites, but I love them both the same.

"Where's my hug?" I ask, grabbing Lily's attention.

"Aunty Violet!" she squeals, running toward me. She hugs my legs, and I bend down to her level to give her a proper hug. I squeeze her tight and kiss the top of her head. "Do you want to pick flowers with us?" she asks me in her adorable little voice.

"I would love to, sweetie, but I have to visit with uncle Marco and your daddy first—maybe after?" I tell her, smiling down at her.

"Okay!"

She runs back to the flower bed. Sabrina and I both watch her.

She turns to me. "Marco mentioned you were coming for a visit; I guess it turned into business?" she asks with a smirk.

"When is it not with those two?"

"I take it that means you won't be staying long?"

"Probably not, but I promise I'll come visit again soon, and we can have a girls' night."

"I've been dying for one of those, and I know Nikki is, too." She smiles.

"Perfect, then we'll set it up. Hey, where's Midnight?" I ask, turning my head around looking for him.

Midnight is Sabrina's Cane Corso; he's a beast of a dog, but a sweetheart when he likes you and knows you're not a threat. He's usually watching Sabrina like a hawk and is glued to her side.

"I left him with my mother back home, I think he's getting tired of flying." She laughs. "Can't say I blame him, I am, too, at this point." Sabrina gives me a soft smile. "You should take a break, get the girls at the helpline to take on more jobs."

"No, I'm fine, really, it's just been a busy few weeks, that's all."

She gives me a look. "Okay, if you say so, but if you need me to tell my husband off for you, I will," she says, trying to sound serious.

"Ha, no need, I have no problem telling him off myself, you know that. I'm fine, honestly," I reassure her. "I better go see them, we'll talk later."

"Sounds good," she replies. "Good luck."

"Thanks," I say, rolling my eyes and smirking at her.

I head back inside and walk down the hall to Marco's office. One of Marco's men, Rocco, is guarding his office door. Marco always has someone guard his office when discussing Mafia business, to make sure no one disrupts him. Rocco greets me and opens the African Blackwood doors. I thank him and enter the office. Both Dante and Marco are sitting in lounge chairs by the fire. The space represents Marco so well; it's dark and moody but also has a cozy feel, too—much like him.

He has a drink in his hand, the amber liquid shining from the light of the fire. There's two folders on the coffee table in front of them. They both turn their heads to me, neither of them looking too stressed, so I'm hoping this isn't as serious as I thought.

Marco stands to give me a hug. "Hello, piccola salvatrice."

Marco's nickname for me is 'little savior.' I've learned some Italian from him and Dante, but I can understand it better than I can speak it. Dante calls me either 'Red' or 'V.' It used to annoy me, but they've sorta grown on me.

"Ciao, fra," I say back to him.

Marco smiles, but it doesn't quite reach his eyes. Shit, maybe I was wrong—by his expression, this meeting seems more serious now. He gestures for me to take a seat in the chair in the middle, and I do so, enjoying the warmth from the fire. Marco has this place like an ice box half the time, so it's nice sitting in a room and having it actually be warm.

"So, what's going on? Who do I have to kill?" I ask with a smirk.

"Oh, you're gonna enjoy killing this one, Red," Dante says with a mischievous look.

"Am I?" I raise a brow. "Well don't keep me in suspense any longer, who is he?" I ask.

"It won't be just one, unfortunately." Marco sighs. "I will admit this one pains me to say... It's a priest." Marco looks visibly distraught.

"You've got to be shitting me," I say.

"Told you you would enjoy this one," Dante chimes in.

He's right. Now, I have no hate for priests... Well, not all priests. And I have no problem with religion unless they shove it down people's throats and use it for power—which a lot of Catholics do. The Catholic church has more ghosts and secrets than any other religion I know. Marco is somewhat of a religious man, so to need me to kill a priest for him must mean he did something unforgivable.

"It seems Father Raymond has strayed from his Holy duties," Marco says.

"Yes, he certainly has. The figlio di puttana is raping and trafficking young women—very young," Dante seethes, clenching his teeth. Marco's accent is stronger than Dante's, but when Dante is mad, his Italian really shows.

My next question is hard to ask, but I need to know. "How old?"

Marco breathes deeply, trying to keep himself calm. He would love nothing more than to flip this coffee table right into the fire; Mafia men aren't the best at controlling their tempers.

"Some were 17, some 15." He pauses. "The youngest was 13."

The hitch in his voice at the mention of the 13 year old makes me uneasy. My knuckles crack from clenching my fists so tight. I look at Dante, whose face appears sad, instead of the anger that was there just moments ago, and I know what that means. It never gets easier hearing about the women I saved, and what they've gone through, but it's hardest when it's one I couldn't save. They can't all be rescued, but maybe others could have if I had only found out they needed my help sooner.

"What happened to her?" I ask.

"You tell her, brother; I can't without flying over there right now and killing him myself," Dante says, practically spitting venom after each syllable.

"We think she tried to escape. My sources tell me witnesses saw a girl running out of his church late at night into the forest, with men chasing after her." Marco has connections, and these "sources" as he calls them are essentially men—and sometimes women—he's hired to scope out different areas he believes may have high trafficking. "When people at the church asked the priest about the girl and what those witnesses had seen that night, he played it off like she was a troubled teen who was into drugs and alcohol, that they were trying to help her, but she ran off."

Fucker. Of course they all believed him.

Marco opens up one of the files on the table and hands me a photo from it. "Her name was Isabella," he tells me.

I stare at the photo of her—her smile, her light-brown hair. Closing my eyes, I see her, running scared as if I'm right there with her. Everything she must have felt in that moment floods through me; her feet burning from running for her life, the pain in her chest from running out of breath and not knowing what comes next if she stops. I do this often, vividly placing myself in the scene the woman was in—it helps make the killing easier. Channeling their pain, their fear.

I open my eyes, and my brothers are staring at me, my face plastered in anger. "Where is he? Where do I have to go?"

"Home. Well, your old home," Dante replies.

"He's trafficking women in Canada!? And he hasn't been caught yet?" I yell, not understanding how something like this could get missed.

"He's very good at playing the friendly neighborhood priest, and when anyone questions him about suspicious activity in the church, he has an excuse —they're all blind to his charm," Marco sneers.

Of course they are, why am I not surprised?

"The men that work with him pretend to be a late night AA group, so to the outside world, they're recovering alcoholics who have found God and the church, when really, they are traffickers who found an easy way to abuse girls undetected," Marco explains. "In a way, it's smart; some of these girls are part of the church, and some are runaways or escorts who are looking to be saved and think the church is a safe place. But once they get in, they're trapped."

"It's fucking diabolical," Dante spits.

My blood boils listening to them, and it's about to get worse once I ask my next question. "How did they kill her?" I ask, barely audible.

Dante stands. "You guys finish this meeting, I need to help Nikki get Lily ready for her swimming lessons, and I rather not hear this."

Understandable—Dante's been more sensitive to the trafficking talks since getting married and having a daughter.

"You're staying for dinner, right, V?" Dante asks.

"Sure, I'll leave tonight," I reply. He nods and leaves the room. "So, how did they murder her?" I ask again.

Marco looks into the fire and lifts his drink to take a sip. "They burned her. I don't know if she was still alive when they did it, but I assume he wanted to use her as an example to the other girls, to show what happens when they run."

"Are you sure she was burned?" I ask, wanting to know for sure.

"Yes. One of my sources snuck into the forest behind the church, to see if she was still hiding, but all he found was a pile of ash with crushed bone fragments in it."

I look away from the fire. Well, I guess I've picked how Father Raymond will die.

"You will take a few of my men with you. It's not a request," Marco demands.

I roll my eyes at him. *Overprotective much?*

"Fine, I could always use the extra muscle," I tease, winking at him.

"Good, I'll make sure the plane's ready for you tonight. Now go spend some time with my wife, she's been complaining that I've been keeping you from her the last few times you've visited."

We both stand. "Oh, don't worry, she's already tried to lecture me about working too much," I tell him.

"She's not wrong. If you need a break, all you have to do is say," Marco assures me.

"I know, I'm good," I promise him.

"Hmm, whatever you say, piccola salvatrice."

I smile at him. Marco knows me too well now. I might be good at hiding my emotions and the fact I'm dying on the inside, but Marco knows when I'm bullshitting now; he's caught onto my signs.

"Tell Sabrina I'll be down in a few minutes, I just wanna change into comfy clothes and pack a few things for my long flight tonight."

As if on cue, Sabrina yells Marco's name through the mansion.

"Coming, piccola diavolo!" Marco yells back to her.

I laugh at him as he leaves me to go find her. The Berlusconi men sure love their nicknames. I go upstairs to my bedroom. There's some clothes here already for when I visit—makes it easier than lugging them back and forth. I go through my closet, throwing clothes in my suitcase, already knowing the perfect outfit to kill Father Raymond in. Just because I'm killing a man doesn't mean I can't look good doing it.

A black blazer with beautiful embroidery on the sleeves, and matching dress pants. And for underneath, I pack a black, mesh, long-sleeve top with a cross down the front; how fitting for a church event. Once I'm all packed, I flop down on my bed. considering a nap before dinner. I'm exhausted from my flight, and my emotions are making me more tired. I shut my eyes, thinking about killing Father Raymond tomorrow. You reap what you sow,

Father Raymond, and I am the reaper coming to collect.

Galatians 6:7

Do not be deceived, God is not mocked; for whatever a man sows, this he will also reap.

CHAPTER 5
Going To Hell

Violet

GOD, I HATE churches. Don't get me wrong, I appreciate the beauty and craftsmanship of a church, but I still hate them nonetheless. For most people, churches bring peace, salvation and holiness. For me, they bring disgust, anger and bitterness toward the many people that run them. People like good ol' Father Raymond.

I've brought a few of Marco's men with me—an order, not a request—but I don't mind the help this time, seeing as how I'll be needing them for some heavy lifting. I smirk up at the entrance to the church, its tall wooden doors with brass handles on each side. The doors display engravings, and beautifully etched vines and symbols mirror the handles. It looks as though someone carved them by hand. It's almost a shame I'll be burning it down. Almost. Excitement and angst battle each other in my stomach.

I turn to Marco's men behind me, a few of them still grabbing our supplies from the car. "You ready, guys?" I ask them.

They all say, "Yes, ma'am," and wait for me to open the doors. I place my hand on the metal handle, warm from the sun; it's almost sunset, but the remaining sunlight is strong. The doors fly open from the force and I walk inside. Four greasy men practically jump out of the pews they were sitting in and turn toward me, their faces mirroring each other with shock. One of them decides to finally talk while the others just stare.

"Sorry, lady, church is closed. It's only open on Sundays and Mondays for confessional."

I smile at the man and put on my best sad girl act. "Oh no, really? That's too bad, my friends and I were looking forward to confessing our sins."

Marco's men flank me. Father Raymond's buddies practically shit their pants when they see them. Two of them move farther back into the church near the altar, as if that will somehow protect them from us, which has me laughing to myself. This is one of my favorite parts about my job; watching men who prey on innocent women and children cower in fear when they meet someone who is much bigger and stronger than them; it fills me with so much joy.

"I guess since we can't confess our sins, we'll just have to act on them," I say, continuing the sweet, innocent girl approach, smiling at them all.

The same man that spoke out earlier speaks again. "What the fuck is this? Who the fuck are you people?"

I put a hand on my chest, mimicking shock and suck in a breath. "My goodness, such language in a house of God. I would think you would know better, especially for a man who spends most of his weekends here. Isn't that right, fellas?"

Dropping the act now, I look at the men with a straight face. "Now, tell me, do your families know you picked up a hobby on the weekends involving bringing young women to a church so you can rape them?" I ask, sick to my stomach.

They stare at each other, shocked that I know their dirty little secret.

When none of them answer, I continue, "No? Wow, I'm surprised that's something you wouldn't wanna share with them," I say sarcastically.

"What do you want from us? Why are you here?" stammers one of the men whose hiding behind the altar and has decided to grow some balls.

The man beside him speaks first before I get a chance to answer his questions. "You here to rid us of our sins?" he asks, laughing. The other three men laugh along with him.

God, these fucking men are so stupid; wait until they realize how much shit they're really in and that their lives are about to be mine in five seconds.

I straighten my back and glare at them. "No, I'm not here to rid you of your sins; your sins are yours to bear. I'm here for revenge, and to make sure you disgusting pieces of shit never hurt anyone ever again."

My smirk diminishes, left with pure anger and hatred in its place. The men have now all changed their tune, no longer laughing. They're just as pissed off as I am, maybe even a little disgusted now in my presence. *Join the club, assholes.* This has dragged on long enough, and the longer I'm near these men, the more my blood boils, and Father Raymond will be arriving soon.

"I think I'm done answering questions," I say, snapping my fingers to signal Marco's men to get to work .

They move toward the four men, grabbing each one. These pricks try to fight, but sadly for them, Marco's men are much stronger, and more pissed off. It's kinda funny watching them struggle. I laugh to myself, watching them take the men to the back room that leads to the stairs for the balcony of the church. With the distraction gone, I take a minute to examine the church—its walls, stained glass windows, with murals of Jesus and the angels. It's an older church; the stench of mold and mildew is thick in the air.

I decide to take a seat and wait for my special guest to arrive. Suddenly, the church fills with the screams of Father Raymond's men. Normally, I wouldn't miss out on a good kill, especially one of those scumbags, but I'm saving all my pent-up killing energy for Father Raymond. So until then, I'll just sit tight and enjoy the sounds of his men dying.

THE CHURCH DOORS open behind me; Father Raymond has finally arrived, and now the real fun can begin. I light another Votive candle, the sixth candle I've lit. Their bright-red wax starts to pool at the top and drip down the sides, reminding me of all the blood I'm about to spill on these church floors.

Father Raymond's footsteps approach, deeper into the church, my back still to him. He stops abruptly, finally noticing I'm here. He probably thinks I'm a little surprise his friends have left him, their next victim to play with. Good—it will make it so much sweeter when he realizes it's the other way around.

The candles flicker as I stare at the flames. "Hello, Father," I call out to him.

He clears his throat. "Forgive me, I didn't realize anyone was here, the church is supposed to be closed."

I turn to face him, smiling. His dark-brown hair is slightly disheveled, but besides that, he looks like the perfect priest he pretends to be. I walk closer to him. He's standing in the middle of the church, pews on either side, and I stop about five feet from him.

"I'm sorry if I'm intruding, Father, but I'm afraid I have an important matter I need to speak with you about."

My voice is etched with concern, making him think I'm here to confess all my dirty little secrets. He looks me up and down, a slow, predatory movement; it's amazing how fast men like him can flip like a switch.

"Of course, I am here to help all of God's children, especially those who need it most," he says with a half-hearted smile that doesn't reach his eyes.

God's children my ass. Fuck, I can't wait to kill this son of a bitch!

He gestures for me to walk in front of him and toward the confessionals. "Please."

I don't move from where I'm standing. "Oh, no, Father. You're mistaken. I'm not here to confess my sins—I'm here for yours."

He looks at me, confused. "I-I'm sorry, I don't understand."

I smirk at him. "Oh, you will soon." I walk toward the altar and lean against it. "You see, Father, it's no secret what you use this church for, besides bible study and Sunday Mass. In fact, I'd bet there's more unholiness that happens inside its walls than outside of them."

Father Raymond scowls at me, his confusion turning into anger. "I don't know what you think you're accusing me of—"

I cut him off before he has time to spew more bullshit, and get right to the point. "How many women have you raped and sold in this church, Father?"

If the mix of fury and disgust on my face could kill, he'd already be dead. I'm curious to know his answer, even though I know the correct one already. Surprisingly, he looks more shocked than angry that he's been caught. His next statement throws me off a little.

"How dare you! Get the hell out of my church!" He starts moving closer to me and pointing to the entrance.

Attempting to hold back my laughter by placing a hand over my mouth, a small giggle spills out. "I'm sorry, Father, I don't mean to laugh, but seeing you so angry and thinking you have the upper hand here is downright comical."

He puts his hand down, fuming now, which makes me want to laugh harder.

He steps closer. "If you don't leave right this instant, I'll be forced to—"

"Forced to do what exactly, Father?" I ask him, raising one eyebrow and crossing my arms.

Grinding his teeth, his frustration is obvious. He straightens his shoulders. "I have men coming here soon."

"Oh, you mean your little rapist friends?" I tilt my head slightly. "Yeah, I've already met them. Now that you mention it, why don't we have them join us as well?"

I place two fingers between my lips and whistle, signaling Marco's men. They come through the balcony doors of the church one by one, dragging

Father Raymond's men with them. Marco's men drop the bodies over the side of the balcony, nooses tied around their necks. The ends of the ropes are tied to wooden spindles, securing them in place.

I glance down to look at Father Raymond, his eyes now filled with fear. I smile at him. "Now do you understand, Father?" My voice moves his attention away from the balcony and back to me. I slowly walk toward him, never breaking eye contact. "The Devil sent me, Father." Each step I take, he takes one back. "He sent me here to clean up your mess and take solace in your suffering."

Father Raymond's back hits one of the church pews. The predatory, confident man from earlier has vanished, and he lifts his hands up in surrender. "P-please," he stutters.

I laugh right in the fucker's face and reach into my back pocket for my brass knuckles, placing them over my fingers. "Oh, Father, your pleas mean absolutely fucking nothing to me!" I spit, gripping the metal tightly.

I swing with all my strength and slam the brass knuckles into his head. He crumples to the floor, unconscious. Marco's men join me.

I look at Rocco. "Tie him up to that chair over there." I nod in the direction of the wooden chair in the far corner.

"Yes, ma'am," he says while nodding back to me.

I roll my eyes. It's annoying when Marco's men call me ma'am, but I get it's a respect thing, it just makes me feel like someone's grandma.

Rocco grabs Raymond's body, throwing it over his shoulder like he weighs nothing and carries him to the chair that has now been placed in the middle of the church. I follow him and watch as he drops Raymond into it, tying up his legs and arms. He wraps one final rope around his chest to stop him from being able to move his shoulders. Tony drops a bag on the bench behind me, containing various objects that I've packed to torture Father Raymond with.

There's a small golden bowl on a stand near the altar I noticed earlier, which I believe to be holy water. I take the one step to the altar toward it; there's engravings of crosses along the sides, giving me a clear indication that it is indeed holy water. I pick the bowl up off the stand and carry it down to where Raymond sits. Standing in front of him, bowl in hand, I survey the church, making sure each one of Marco's men are stationed where they need to be—two guarding the entrance, one beside me on my right and another behind Raymond's chair. Perfect.

Satisfied, I lift the bowl of holy water and splash some onto Father Raymond's face, waking him. He squints his eyes and tries to spit out some of the water that trickled into his mouth.

"Good morning, Father, did you have a nice little nap?" I ask sarcastically.

His vision finally clears, and he looks down at himself, realizing just how fucked he really is. "W-what's happening? Untie me, now!" he yells.

I sigh. "Come on now, Father, do you really think that's going to happen? After Rocco went through all that trouble, military-knotting your restraints?" I look at him questioningly. "I think not, so let's stop with the useless demands and pleas, because they won't save you, Father—I'm afraid nothing will."

I turn my back to him for a second while I grab a knife from my bag. It's different from my usual throwing knives; it's a lot bigger with a jagged blade. Turning back to face him, I closely inspect the blade. Very carefully, I run my finger across its jagged edge. Raymond widens his eyes, looking like he might piss himself.

"Now, we're gonna play a little game, because why not make this more fun? Well, more fun for me—not so much you." My frown is fake as fuck. "I'm going to ask you some questions; questions I know the answers to, and each time you lie, or don't answer, I take a piece of your flesh."

I bring the knife to his face, taunting him with it. Trembling like a little bitch, he looks up at the ceiling and starts mumbling prayers to himself. *Seriously? He's gotta be joking.* He begs God for forgiveness, and a laugh bursts out of me. Moving closer to him, his knees now touching my upper thighs, I reach over and wrap my hand around his throat, choking him, forcing his head down so we are eye to eye.

"Go ahead, Father, ask him for absolution. You think he will give it to you?" I ask, anger lacing my tone. "If there really is a God up there, what makes you think he gives two shits about you? Because you spread his Gospel, hmm? Pretend to be a man of faith." Squeezing his throat harder, I watch him choke on each breath he tries to take. "In fact, I think he would praise *me* for all the work I've done, and for taking it upon myself to take his trash out for him."

When Father Raymond's face starts turning purple, I release him. I straighten my back and loom over him while he coughs as he takes in a lungful of air.

"How many women have you raped and trafficked in this church?" I ask him while holding my knife lazily in my hand, waiting for his answer.

But no words spill out. I roll my eyes at him; clearly, Father Raymond thinks I'm bluffing. You would think almost choking him to death would have sent the message that I'm not to be fucked with. I guess I'll have to do better. Bringing the knife to his thigh, I press the blade into his skin, agonizingly slow. He thrashes in the chair, but the bindings keep him secured. Trickles of blood begin to seep from the wound and down his leg.

He wails in pain as I press my knife harder into his skin and repeat the question. "I don't answer to you!" he grunts.

"Wrong answer, asshole," I snap, slicing the blade across his skin, leaving a gaping gash in its wake. He screams, and satisfaction blooms across my face. "I could do this all night, Father. I enjoy inflicting pain on those who deserve it, and trust me when I say you. Do. Deserve it!" I punctuate each word, then turn to his left thigh, ready to do the same to it.

He shakes violently, in obvious pain. "Please, no!" he shouts, breathing heavily and still fighting the ropes.

"This could all be avoided, Father, if you just answer my simple question."

I'm lying, of course; whether he answers my questions or not, I'm going to kill him. I'm enjoying letting him think I won't, letting him hope that if he complies, I'll let him go. The same hope the women felt after he was done raping them.

As I press the tip of the blade into his skin again, he squeezes his eyes shut, sweat dripping down his face. "S-six," he stutters.

I smile up at him. "There, was that so hard?" I say condescendingly.

I lift the blade away from his thigh, and he stops tensing, the slightest touch of relief on his face. But it doesn't last long. I plunge my knife into his leg, feeling it go through each layer of skin and sinewy flesh. His screams of agony echo throughout the church, sounding better than any gospel I've ever heard. I made sure to aim for a spot with no major arteries so he won't bleed out. We can't have him die too soon, not when I've only just started. My knife now protrudes from his thigh, allowing enough blood to paint the church floors crimson.

Father Raymond looks about ready to pass out but musters up enough strength to keep talking. "I don't understand, I answered your question," he breathes out.

"No, you lied, Father! I told you I know the truth, yet you chose to lie anyway; you brought this pain on yourself," I seethe angrily. "The correct answer is ten. Ten innocent women you defiled with your disgusting fucking hands and your shriveled up dick!"

I could vomit just looking at him. He's pale, either from blood loss or my words, though honestly, it could be both. "Then once you were done using them as your own personal toy, you sold them to the highest bidder.

What happened, Father, the church not bringing in enough donations for you?" I question him.

"You don't understand, I-I saved them, those women were sinners!" he says with great anger, and a scowl on his face.

"And what? You thought you were purifying them with your cock? No, Father, you saw an opportunity to use your position of power to feed on your own sick desires. You didn't give a shit about these women or their sins, that much is true."

I look to my right toward Rocco, making eye contact with him. I shift my eyes toward the metal rod resting on the lectern, and he nods, walking to go grab it. He returns holding it, and I reach out to grab it from him, the metal cooling my heated hand as I grip the handle. Rocco moves to stand behind Raymond's chair and places his hands on his shoulders.

Raymond moves his head frantically side to side. "What are you doing?" he says in a panic.

I lift the metal rod, showing him exactly what it is. His eyes widen when he sees the arms of the crucifix at the base. "You used this to brand the women, like fucking cattle! Marking them so they would forever remember what you did to them!" I say, enraged.

Nico hands me a small blow torch from one of our bags. I light it and place the metal crucifix brand under the blue-orange flame, watching it heat up.

"Oh god, please, no! Haven't I suffered enough?" Father Raymond yells.

I ignore his plea, and turn the blow torch off once the crucifix turns red with scorching heat. I walk closer toward him so our knees are flush once again.

"I think for you, Father, it's only fitting that I brand you with this cross upside down, seeing as how you will no longer be serving God, but becoming Satan's bitch, instead."

I lift the brand to his forehead. He tries to move his head, but Rocco holds him in place for me as I press the brand into his skin as hard as I can, searing his flesh. The sound of the metal burning into it sounds exactly like pressing down on a meat patty on the grill and hearing it sizzle, which is oddly satisfying. You know, in a sick sorta way.

I expect Father Raymond to scream, but he merely grunts and clenches his teeth in pain. His body must be numb from shock and losing blood. I release the brand from his head and drop the metal to the floor, stepping back and admiring my work. The skin around the inverted crucifix is raised, red and angry-looking. Inside it, welts have started to form from the burn.

Rocco lets go of his head and it lolls to one side, his body giving up the fight. Now's the perfect time to end this; the revenge isn't half as sweet once they give up and pass out.

"Nico, Rocco, grab the gas canisters," I order them.

"Finally, I'm getting hungry," Nico says.

I laugh and shake my head at him. Of course all he's thinking about is food at a time like this. They start pouring gasoline around the church, leaving a clear path to the front for us to walk out. They make their way to where I'm standing and start pouring gas on Father Raymond's head, jostling his attention back to me. He spits gas weakly. I grab him by his hair, now soaked from the gasoline and prop his head up so we're eye to eye. I want my eyes to be the last thing he sees before I burn him alive.

"Stay awake for me, Father, I have one last thing to say to you before you meet your end."

"What did you pour on me? It smells like gas!" he shouts.

"That's because it is, Father. This is the final act of revenge. I'm burning you and this church is going down with you. I choose this as your way of dying for Isabella. You remember her, don't you father? The girl you burned for trying to escape? Your body will be nothing but ash and dust once anyone finds you, just like she was." I release him and back away. "Oh, I almost forgot this."

I look down at the knife still protruding out of his thigh. I grip the handle and pull it out. He grunts, and more blood starts to flow out of the hole now that it's exposed. I wipe the blood off onto his shirt and throw the knife into my bag, zipping it up. One of Marco's men come up beside me.

"We good to go, Violet?" he asks.

I nod and turn my back to Father Raymond and walk toward the exit. I stop halfway and turn around to face him again. Reaching into my pocket for my zippo lighter, I flick it open. Father Raymond looks at me, his eyes slightly squinted. He may not be able to hear me, but I say one last goodbye to him, a saying that I've heard Marco say to his enemies once before.

"Che il diavolo si nutra della tua anima e ti torturi all'inferno per tutta l'eternità."

May the devil feed on your soul and torture you in hell for all eternity.

I throw the lighter into the gasoline and watch as it catches flame, making its way to Father Raymond. He screams a blood-curdling scream as the flames engulf him. I turn and walk out the door, leaving him and the pain and suffering of those women behind. Hopefully, they will be able to have some peace with him gone.

Nico closes the door behind me, placing a metal lock chain around the handles. Smoke starts to seep through the roof of the church. We make our way back to the vehicle. Rocco opens the door for me and we all get in. Relaxing into the seat and the buzz from killing Father Raymond wearing off, my stomach starts to rumble, and I realize I, too, am hungry.

"Who's up for burgers?"

CHAPTER 6
The Russian

Violet

AS MUCH AS I love Canada, being back home even for a day brings back too many bad memories from my past. Which is why I don't go back often, but when I do, I always have these flashback dreams. It varies between visions of scenes with my mother. Sometimes with exes too, but mostly her and my childhood. I'm glad I hopped on the plane with Marco's men for New York last night after we grabbed a bite to eat. I was going to stay an extra day and visit some of my favorite places but decided last minute against it. I thought after years of these nightmares, they would end, but I guess that's the beauty of childhood trauma. It sticks with you forever, no matter how hard you try to get rid of it.

You would think a woman like me who does what I do would have different types of nightmares. Ones with guilt, and the men I've killed screaming out in pain. But no. Besides the childhood trauma and mommy-issue nightmares, I sleep pretty well. I'm sure there's some fucked up reason behind it all, but I dont care to know it. As long as I can keep saving women and making them feel at peace, I will. Maybe one day I will feel shame for the things I've done, but until then, I will continue to rid the earth of the men who no longer deserve to be on it.

I sit up in my bed and turn my bedside lamp on, rubbing the sleep from my eyes and grab my phone off the charger. 7:30 a.m. Not bad, I guess. I might as well start my day early even though I really don't have much to do. Beats trying to fall back to sleep just to get woken up again by my lovely mother's psychotic face. As I'm about to climb out of bed, my phone rings.

Natalia's contact, one of the women that works for me, flashes on my screen.

"Hey, what's up? Everything okay?" I ask.

"Hey, yeah, sorry to call you so early, we got a call last night from a woman who needs help. She said her name is Mary. I'm not sure if that is her real name or not; she didn't give a last name, but sounded terrified."

I sigh. "Okay, did she say why?"

"Well, she didn't give us much information, just said her boyfriend beats her and that she's scared he might kill her."

"Did she give his name?" I ask.

"First name only—Igor."

What a stupid fucking name. "Okay, see what you can find on him and take care of it," I say, slightly annoyed.

I don't mind when Natalia calls me, but for something as simple as this, it wasn't necessary. We frequently get calls from scared wives and girlfriends about their significant others beating on them. They're our number one callers, which is fucked up, but hey, so is life. I'm just confused as to why she felt the need to call me about this one.

"Well, there's one more thing..." she says before she hangs up, "which is the reason for my call." She mentioned that he may or may not be in the Russian Mob.

"Fuck, of course he is, I should have known with a stupid name like that that he was a meathead who worked for the Russian Bratva." I grit my teeth. "I'll handle it, just send me whatever you found and get a guard to secretly watch her place to ensure her safety until I get this sorted."

"Sounds good, and good luck," she says and hangs up.

I sigh again and rub my face. This makes things a little more complicated, and I understand Natalia reaching out to me now. Normally, she could handle this on her own, but when it involves someone in the criminal organization or political world, it needs to go through me. The Italians and Russians have made peace in New York; I wouldn't say they're friends by any means, but they have made a peace treaty of sorts over the years, and part of that treaty is if someone on either side has an issue with a man in their gang, the two heads of the Mafia have a meeting about it and decide the proper punishment for that person.

Meaning I can't very well show up to Igor's house and kill him myself. I have to either go through Marco or try and have my own meeting myself with Viktor Andreyevich and let him take care of Igor. But she called my Help Line, and Marco's been too busy dealing with a mess in Italy. I don't want to get him involved just yet, so I guess I have no choice but to pay Viktor—the head of the Russian Bratva here in New York—a visit.

We have never met, but Marco has kept me up to date with all the gangs and criminal leaders here, and had mentioned one time that he owns a Russian-themed nightclub downtown called Sem' Chertey Russkiy, which I believe means 'Seven Devils.'

The only information I know about Viktor is that he's forty-two and has been the head of the Andreyevich Bratva since he was eighteen, after his father's death. It's been said that he's a ruthless, brutal man—like most men in the mafia. Besides that, I have no idea what kind of man I will be dealing with, but one thing's for sure: if Viktor doesn't say he will take care of Igor himself, I will. Consequences be damned.

Later that evening, I'm getting ready to head to Viktor's club. It's been awhile since I've been to one, so I thought I would try and dress up a little, seeing as how I don't get out much these days. Unless it involves killing a man, and call me crazy, but I do enjoy looking nice while killing, and I have a feeling I could end up killing one of Viktor's guards if they try to give me any trouble.

I go with a simple black dress with bell sleeves, nylons since it's a cooler night, and a pair of knee-high black boots. I put a few waves in my hair to give it more volume and keep my makeup the same as I usually do. One last mirror check before I grab my black leather jacket and purse to leave, but before I do, I slip one of my throwing knives into my thigh strap that's placed over my tights. Just in case I need it. I never go anywhere without at least one knife on me. I texted Maison earlier today and told him the plan and to pick me up at 10:30 p.m. to take me to the club. I could have just called an uber, but I wanted him there in case shit hits the fan. You never know with these Mafia men, especially the Russians.

I've learned from Marco not to trust any of them, no matter how convincing they may seem; all these men are the same. Truce or not, they still can't be trusted. Sure, my name gives me a layer of protection against them, and if they were smart, they would know not to fuck with me, but there's always some fucker who thinks he's above the rules and is a real tough ass with a need to prove it. And yes, I'm good at what I do. I've trained to kill a man in ten seconds, but a room full of hundreds of Russian Mafia men? Well, like I said, I'm good but not that good.

I meet Maison out front and climb into his car. "Hey, sunshine, you ready to kill some Russian gangsters?" he asks with a boyish smile.

I give him an eye roll. "No killing, just talking," I reassure him.

"Right," he replies sarcastically. "We'll see."

I shake my head and smile as we head downtown.

MAISON DROPS ME off in front of the club and goes to find a parking spot. I tell him I will call or text if I need him. I walk along the sidewalk up to the club. The thumping of music outside is loud, and there's a huge lineup of people trying to get in that circles around the block. Who knew there were so many Russians—or people who like Russian music—in New York? There's two big, muscular guards posted in front of the main entrance; both look more like bodybuilders than bouncers.

I ignore the front entrance and make my way to the back alley entrance the staff use. There's another muscled meathead blocking the door, whose muscles are just as big as the other two. I make my way to him, and he looks at me with a mean grimace on his face, clearly not happy to see me. That makes two of us.

"The front entrance is that way," he says in a thick Russian accent while pointing back to where I came from.

"Yes, I know, I'm here to see Viktor. My name is Violet Berlusconi," I say sternly.

His upper lip raises in disgust at the mention of my name, and he lifts his microphone attached to his shirt. He mouths off something in Russian then waits for a response.

"Da," he says back, which I know means "Yes" or "Okay." He steps to the side and opens the door for me. "He will be waiting for you in the VIP lounge."

I look him up and down. "Thanks," I say, unenthused.

He grunts back at me, and I continue through the door into the club. Bright-red fluorescent lights illuminate the inside, momentarily obstructing my vision. I make my way further into the club, my eyes finally adjusting to the red lights as I take in the ugly furniture and wall decor with tacky Russian patterns and symbols. *Wow, they really went hard on the Russian theme.* Russian rap music thumps through the speakers and gets louder the deeper I make my way into the club.

A group of Russian men are sitting at a table playing poker, and they eye me with dirty looks as I walk past. One of them goes as far as to place his gun on the table to make sure I see it. I smirk at them to let them know they don't scare me. They're probably Viktor's men; he must have let them know I was here and to keep an eye on me. Silly men. There isn't one man in this club that I would ever be afraid of. I've met men far worse than them—and killed them, too.

I make my way to the dance floor as men and women dance and grind on each other to the beat of the music. At the end, there's women dancing in cages, swaying their hips and flipping their hair back and forth. The VIP lounge is up ahead with a rope and a guard out front blocking its access. *There you are, Viktor.* The faster I talk to him, the faster I can get out of this hideous club. It's not that the music is bad or even the wallpaper. It's more these red lights. It looks more like a sex club you would find at the Red Light District in Amsterdam.

I push my way through the crowd, trying to get the least amount of their sweat as possible on me and push my way to the front of the VIP lounge. I walk up the four steps and meet the guard at the top. He eyes me suspiciously.

"Violet Berlusconi," I announce, and he nods, removing the rope and allowing me inside.

Men are laughing to my right and I turn toward them. Four of them sit on a black leather couch with a glass coffee table in front. My breath catches when I see the man sitting in the middle, smoking a cigar. He takes a puff of it, and I watch as he inhales then releases the smoke into the air. Viktor. This is the first time I've seen him in person. I've seen photos of him but didn't pay much attention.

Turns out he's hot. Like, really hot... Which kinda pisses me off, and I'm not sure why. I can appreciate a fine man when I see one. Just because I kill men for a living and haven't dated or slept with one in years doesn't mean I don't find certain men attractive. But finding him of all people hot pisses me off. Maybe it's because in a way, I see him as the enemy, even though Marco has no beef with him. Or maybe it's because I'm only here to see him because one of his asshole men is a woman-beater. Either way, I don't like how I feel when I look at him.

Viktor makes eye contact with me. He gives me a smoldering look that makes him even more attractive and beckons me forward, closer to him. My body moves on instinct, and I need to keep reminding myself why I'm here and keep my face free of emotions. I stand in front of him, the coffee table the only barrier between us. His face clearer now, my eyes zero in on his jaw line, the tightly trimmed hair on his face. He has a few small scars—on his forehead and across his cheeks. Dirty-blond hair is cut short on the sides. The men sitting next to him stop talking, and they all focus on me. I pay them no attention, keeping my eyes locked on Viktor. He slowly looks me up and down and smirks at me.

"Violet Berlusconi, it's nice to finally meet you," he says, his voice deep with a slight Russian accent.

"The feeling's not mutual," I reply, keeping my face blank.

"And why is that?" He is still smirking at me. "Marco and I are on good terms, no? Have I done something to offend you and make you see any different?" he asks.

"Not you, but one of your men has," I say.

Viktor's smirk fades and is now replaced with the same hard look I'm giving him. I didn't see Igor here tonight, and I'm hoping that means Viktor has him running some errand and he's not with Mary.

Viktor looks to his men. "Leave us," he orders while gesturing to them to leave.

They all scatter at Viktor's authoritative tone. It's just Viktor and me now, and I'm suddenly more aware of his dominant aura. It's not fake like a lot of men try to portray. It surrounds me, trying to make me cower and submit to him. *Not happening, Viktor, it won't work on me.*

"So you have an issue with one of my men?" he asks, placing his cigar on the edge of a glass ashtray.

My attention lingers on his hand, his *big* hand… Jesus. It's scarred like his face, and his fingers are adorned with two rings with Russian symbols on them.

"Yes, Igor," I say, moving my attention to his face.

He nods. "Please sit." He gestures to the lounge chair behind me.

"No, thanks, I don't plan on staying long."

He smiles coyly. "What exactly has Igor done?"

"He's been beating the shit out of his girlfriend," I snap. "And I know that may not matter to a man like you, but it does to me, so—"

"A man like me?" he says, cutting me off, which pisses me off again. I wasn't done with my rant. "I may be a man of power, but I do not use that power to beat women, no matter what you may think."

It seems I've pissed him off, too. Good.

"Look, I'm only here because I have to be. If he was any other man, I would have taken care of this by now, but he's yours, so here I am," I say with a condescending tone.

"I didn't know he was seeing someone," he admits.

"Yeah, well, apparently, there's a lot you don't know about the men you hire," I say, not hiding my attitude toward him.

He smirks at me as if he finds my attitude amusing. "I will take care of Igor. Most Russian men are taught from a young age to respect and protect their women, and I am one of those men. I assure you, he will be dealt with."

"Not good enough. I want proof when it's done," I demand, crossing my arms.

"My word is not good enough?" he asks.

"Your word doesn't mean shit to me. You're a man, and men lie, so I need something a little more solid than just your word."

He nods with a sigh. "Fine, I understand. I will send proof to Marco when it's done."

"No, this is my work, not his. You can send the proof to me," I tell him, reaching into my pocket for my card that has the Help Line number on it.

I hand it to Viktor, our fingers slightly brushing against each other and sending tingles throughout my hand. I look up at him and he's staring at me intensely, as if he felt the same thing. I move my hand away quickly and square my shoulders, clearing my throat. He must have just shocked me or something. The card was in my pocket; that explains it.

"I will be in touch," he says.

"Great," I say back, then turn to leave.

"One more thing."

I stop and turn back toward him. He stands and walks around the glass table, now looming over me. Fuck, he's tall. What's with these mafia bosses being so tall? He has to be at least 6'3, maybe even 6'4, and his muscles... It was hard to really see while he was sitting down; they're barely contained in his black dress shirt.

Think of Mary! Stop getting distracted! What the fuck is wrong with me? I never get like this, especially when it comes to men. I almost feel weak. *No!* That feeling can't be right—I'm not weak. Maybe the air in this club is tainted, messing with my mind. I plaster on an annoyed look to stop him from being able to notice the effect he's having on me.

"I would like the name of the woman he hurt," he says with authority.

He's looking right into my eyes as if he's trying to stare into my soul, to try and figure me out. Good luck; all he will find is darkness. The real me is buried deep within it, too far down for anyone to see.

I lift my chin in defiance. "I'm sorry, I can't give that information out. It's confidential."

He raises a brow. "Is it, now? You know you're not the only one with connections. I could find out for myself. I'm asking you out of respect."

"Why do you want her name? So you can pay her off?" I accuse.

He keeps fucking smirking at me, and it's pissing me off. Mainly because it makes him look more attractive, and that annoys me. Why do I keep getting so annoyed by him? I just have to keep telling myself finding Viktor attractive is a big no-no.

"Do I have 'piece of shit' written on my forehead?" he scowls. "I don't want to pay her off. I would like to apologize to her and make sure she is safe."

"I've already made sure of that, and her name is Mary. That's all I'm giving you. I'll expect a text from you tomorrow saying it's done," I say and turn to leave again, not giving him a chance to respond.

Did I do that on purpose so I could have the last word? Yes. Is that childish? Maybe, but right now, I really don't give a shit. I just need to get the hell out of this club and back home. Maybe take a cold shower. At least one thing's for sure: I don't ever have to see Viktor again, and thank god for that.

CHAPTER 7
The Redhead

Viktor

I WATCH HER walk away, staring at her ass in that tight black dress. Not very gentlemanly, but I never said I was one. Her fruity scent still lingers around me, which is aggravating. Violet Berlusconi is a force to be reckoned with. I've heard stories about the many men she's killed, rumors about her hatred for them. I almost didn't believe them until meeting her for the first time tonight. It seems the rumors are true. Not just about that, but her beauty. I can't deny my attraction to her—how could I? With her fiery red hair, full lips and curves... She may hate my sex, but she clearly felt an attraction to me, too.

She's the last woman I thought I would ever see in my club tonight, but our bickering back and forth did make it more interesting. I'm assuming from her tone when I said I would message Marco about Igor that he doesn't know she showed up at my club. Naughty girl. I meant what I said about wanting to make sure this Mary woman is safe. I don't tolerate abusing women in any way, and I'll be damned if I'm going to let that kusok der'ma do it again. No man like that will work for me. I'm a very dangerous man but would never hurt a woman.

I was brought up by both my parents to respect women, and men who abuse them aren't real men. I grew up in Moscow and lived there until I was eighteen, when my father passed. After his death, I moved Mama and myself to New York City; there were better opportunities to grow my father's empire that became mine. I still do business every now and then in Russia, and my family home is still there, and although Mama misses Russia, she's been happier here. She never remarried after my father, and when I had asked her why, she told me my father was her dusha moya.

My father was good to us both. He was hard on me at times, but was raising a strong son that would be the new Packhan one day, and I respect him for it. My mother had fertility issues which is why I am an only child. I have no children of my own and don't want any, nor do I have a wife like most men in the Bratva. Not because I don't want one, but I haven't found the right woman for that role. I've dated, yes, and fucked plenty of women, but I guess I haven't met the woman that matches my soul yet. Perhaps she is here tonight.

"Everything okay, boss?" Alexie, one of my guards, asks.

"Da, find Igor and tell him I need to talk with him in my office," I say.

"Da, Pakhan."

He removes the red velvet rope for me. I walk down the steps and head to my office, two of my other men following on guard behind me. Once inside, they shut the door and guard the outside. I take a seat in my chair and rest my head against it. It's quiet in my office. I had it soundproofed so I can hold meetings here without the noise of the club. My phone lights up on the desk, and my cousin Dimitry's name flashes on the screen.

"Privett, bratt," I answer. *Hello, brother.*

I call Dimitry 'brother' because he is more like one than a cousin.

"Privett, bratt. I have some bad news. I had to take your mother to the hospital. She called me and complained of dizziness. She didn't wanna worry you, but I thought you should know. I am here with her now, and the nurses are running some tests. She has a pretty nasty bump on her head from falling when she got dizzy," he explained.

"Chert!" *Shit.* "Thank you for calling me, I will be there soon."

"Da, do skoroy vstrechi, bratt." *Yes, see you soon, brother.*

I get up and grab my keys off my desk. My mother means the world to me, and I will drop any Bratva business if she needs me. Igor will unfortunately have to wait. I need to see my mama.

I ARRIVE AT Mount Sinai Hospital. It's the best hospital in New York City, and the only one I would trust to take care of my mama. Her health has not been the greatest lately, and she gets these dizzy spells quite frequently. It worries me that she might be getting worse. I will pay and fly in the best doctors in the world to help her, whatever it takes. As I enter her room, Dimitry is standing next to her bed.

"Mama," I call out to her.

She smiles at me as I sit down in the chair closest to her. "Moy krasivyy mal'chik." *My handsome boy.* She grabs my face, kissing my cheek.

"Kak vy sebya chuvstvuyete?" *How are you feeling?*

"Ya v poryadke, golova nemnogo bolit." *I am fine, my head hurts a little.* She touches her head where it hurts.

"I'll get the nurse to give you something."

I go to stand up to get the nurse when my mother puts a hand on my arm to stop me.

"Net net ,ostat'sya," she pleads. "Dimitry will go."

I look to my cousin to see if that is okay. He nods and leaves the room to find a nurse.

I rest a hand on top of hers. "Chto sluchilos', Mama?" *What happened?*

"U menya zakruzhilas' golova, i ya upala, vot i vse." *I felt dizzy and fell, that's all.* She tries to dismiss my worry.

"Vrachu, vozmozhno, pridetsya vypisat' vam novoye lekarstvo, pristupy golovokruzheniya usilivayutsya." *Your doctor may need to prescribe you a new medication, because your dizzy spells are getting worse.*

"Ya zabyla ikh vzyat', ya byla zanyata prigotovleniyem medovika na godovshchinu svad'by tvoikh kuzenov segodnya vecherom." *I forgot to take them, I was busy making honey cake for your cousin's wedding anniversary this evening.*

I frown at her and shake my head, switching to English. "Mama, I told you, I'm having everything catered. You didn't need to make anything."

"But I like to, and what if the dessert is no good? Mine can be backup."

I laugh. "Okay, Mama, but promise me you won't do anymore cooking or baking, you need to rest," I say.

"Ah, please." She waves a hand at me. "You worry too much, Viktor."

"Of course I worry, you are my world, Mama."

"You have too many responsibilities to worry about already." She's referring to my father's empire—*my* empire, now.

"And I would give it all away if you needed me," I promise her.

"Net! Don't be ridiculous, son," she chides.

"So for my sake, Mama, please take your pills."

She kisses my cheek. "Da, moya malen'kaya kapusta." *Yes, my little cabbage.*

I shake my head at the embarrassing nickname she used to call me as a kid. I hated cabbage as a boy, until one day, my father convinced me that it would make me stronger. I was always trying to make him proud, so I would eat handfuls of it whenever I could. One day, I ate so much, I made myself sick, and Mama hasn't ever let me forget it.

Dimitry enters the room with the nurse, and she gives my mother something for the pain, then tells me they would like to keep her overnight to run some more tests. I tell my mother I will stay with her. If I'm going to be here all night, I will need to text Violet and let her know I'll deal with Igor in the morning. She won't be happy, but my family comes first, so she will have to be patient with me—something I feel she's incapable of.

I pull out the business card she gave me at the club and text her personal number. She's most likely still sleeping since it's 2:30 a.m. I would be surprised if she is up, but you never know with a woman like her; she could be off killing a fleet of men right now. I will go see Igor in the morning, have a little chat, maybe cut off his hands for using them to beat a woman, send some pictures to Violet and be on my way. No, maybe I'll tell her to come back to my club to see the evidence in person. That way, I have an excuse to see the red-haired siren again.

CHAPTER 8

Never Trust a Russian

Violet

I WAKE TO two missed messages on my cell phone. One is a missed call from Natalia, and the other is a text. She called me at 3:30 a.m. If she called that late, that means something is wrong. I call her first, before I read my texts.

"Hello?" she answers.

"Hey, I'm sorry I missed your call. I should have had my volume on louder. Is everything—"

She cuts me off. "Mary's in the hospital."

"Fuck! What happened?" I ask.

"Igor found her. I thought you said you took care of him."

"I did! I mean, I thought I did..." Fucking Viktor. That Russian prick lied to me. "What hospital is she at?"

"Harlem Hospital. I'm here with her now. He messed her up pretty bad, Violet," she says quietly.

"Stay with her, I'm coming."

I hang up and get dressed quickly. Remembering I still have a text I haven't read, I grab my phone again and open it. It's from Viktor.

> This is Viktor, something has come up, a family matter. I will deal with Igor in the morning. Don't think I'm blowing this off, I will get it done.

Fucker! Family matter, my ass! I shouldn't have trusted him. Why the fuck did I think I could? Now Mary is in the hospital because I made that mistake. Or worse, she could be in a body bag. Fuming, I grab my keys off the counter and head to the hospital.

I ARRIVE AT the hospital, luckily before the crazy New York traffic. The nurse at the desk tells me which room Mary is in, and there's two police officers talking in the hallway near her room. Great. Thankfully, Marco has a few corrupt cops in his good graces, one of them being a Chief of police. I'll have to give him a call after I'm done with Igor and get him to pretend the cops were never here; the last thing I need is them getting in the way of me killing Igor.

I open the door to Mary's room, and Natalia is standing beside her bed. Shit, Natalia wasn't lying; he did do a number on her. Mary's eyes are nearly swollen shut, with angry purple bruises under them, and a sling around her left arm. Russian piece of shit. As soon as I'm done here, I'm going to Igor's house. Fuck Marco's stupid treaty rules. Viktor didn't follow through with it, so Igor's mine now. Natalia sees me enter and steps aside so I can stand and talk to Mary.

"Mary." I say her name softly so I don't spook her. It's hard to say how much she can see, and I don't want to scare her into thinking just anyone has come in. "I'm Violet, the head of the women's Help Line you called for help. I'm so sorry Igor has done this to you again. I just want you to know, I promise this is the last time he will ever put his hands on you. I trusted someone I shouldn't have to take care of him. None of this was supposed to happen, you were meant to be safe from him," I tell her, ashamed I didn't protect her better. "Natalia will stay by your side while you're in the hospital and some of my team will guard your room."

"No men!" she cries in a weak voice.

"No men. I'll make sure the guards are women only," I reassure her. "Once you are on the mend, you can stay at one of my safe houses if you would like."

"Thank you," she replies, barely audible.

"There's no need to thank me. This is what I do, what I'm supposed to do." I look to Natalia and nod to her, then turn to leave.

"He said he saw you at his boss's club. H-he took my phone and checked my call history. I'm so stupid, I should have deleted it," she cries.

"Hey, it's okay, none of this is your fault. It's mine, but I'm gonna fix it, you just rest and get better."

I storm out of the hospital, and in my car, I text Natalia to send me Igor's address. I didn't want to ask her for it in front of Mary and upset her even more. Once she sends it to me, I forward it to Maison and tell him to scope out Igor's place, then wait for me tonight a few houses down from it. He sends a thumbs-up emoji, and I start my car to head home. Marco will understand, I'll talk with him tomorrow and fill him in on everything. He may be a little disappointed I broke his rules, but at this moment, the only thing I really care about is punishing Igor. As for Viktor, he can fuck off. I made the mistake of thinking he cares, that he is different, but he's just like every other mafia man. I'm not even going to waste my time messaging him back. He can be pissed at me all he wants; I'm pissed at myself for trusting him. There's a long list of men that have disappointed me in my life, and Viktor's name has just been added to it.

I GET A ride from one of Marco's drivers that he has here in New York. He drops me off a few houses down from Igor's. Maison's car is up ahead, and I jog to it. Maison's not inside it, and I can't see him anywhere near Igor's house.

"Boo," Maison whispers right in my ear after sneaking up behind me.

I have a knife in my hand as I turn sharply around to him. "Jesus, Maison! I could have stabbed you!" I hiss.

He gives me a teasing smirk. "Wouldn't be the first time."

I scoff at him. He's referring to the time we were training together, and I cut him by accident. Well, sort of by accident... I mean we were training to fight.

"Is he home?" I ask him.

"Yup, just got in a few minutes ago, must have finished his mafia duties early," he says. "He's alone, no one else has come in or out, and he's got shit security, too. I hacked into his outdoor cameras already and ran the last hour on loop. I guess he thought all those muscles would keep him safe."

"Why do you think I call them meatheads? They have more muscle than brain, and it's not like they need brains, since they're used for running errands or killing. That's about it," I say.

Maison laughs, then looks at me with uncertainty. "You okay? You seem more angry than usual."

"I am. Viktor was supposed to take care of Igor, and because he didn't, Igor nearly killed the woman I was trying to protect from him," I explain.

"Ah shit, no wonder you're pissed. Well, do you want me to go in with you? He's a big guy, you might need my muscles." He winks at me.

I roll my eyes and shake my head at him. "If I need you, I'll signal. You stay out front, make sure we don't get any surprise visitors."

"Yes, Mama, I can do that," he says.

"Great, you got my bag?" I ask.

"Right here," he says, dropping the bag on top of his car's trunk.

I pull out three knives and place them in each sheath I'm wearing. One behind my back, covered by my leather jacket, and the other two in the holsters on either side of my hip. I'm all ready for him.

"If you don't hear him scream, that means I'm dead."

"Roger that," he says, saluting me off.

I give him an unamused look. He's such a dork sometimes. I sneak up along the side of Igor's house. I have my lock kit in my bag, but if Igor's as dumb as I think he is, he probably either left the door unlocked, or a window. I try the front door first; it clicks open. Yup, definitely a dumbass. I quietly open it and enter his house. There's two small lamps on in the living room, leaving the rest of the house pitch black.

For a man that works for the Russian mob, he sure picked a dump to live in. The outside of the house is nice, but the inside is horrid. It's like a bachelor pad mixed with a Russian grandma's house—tacky and cheap-looking. I'm sneaking through the house when my phone vibrates in my pocket, stopping me from going any further. Thinking it could be Maison, I pull it out and open the message. It's Viktor.

> I'm assuming you either didn't get my last message, or you're ignoring me. A shipment of mine was stolen tonight. Once I deal with that, I will deal with Igor. I am sorry for the delay, truly.

This man has excuses coming out his ass! He thinks apologizing will make me any less pissed at him. That may work on other women, but not me. I see right through his bullshit. *God! I would love to punch that man right in his face!* His stupidly handsome face. To think I was even attracted to him... Well, I'm not anymore. An image of him at his club flashes in my mind; his dominance, and that annoyingly sexy smirk he kept giving me. Someone grabs my right shoulder, and my body slams into the living room wall with such force, it knocks the wind out of me.

Fuck! It's Igor. He managed to sneak up behind me while I was distracted by Viktor's stupid text. Igor's meaty, gross hands are around my neck, trying to choke me to death. I gasp for air, but he's crushing my windpipe, not allowing any air in. I reach behind my back for my knife and manage to squeeze it through the small gap between my back and the wall, and jam it into Igor's right shoulder.

"Ugh," he grunts in pain.

While he's distracted by the knife embedded in his shoulder, I kick him as hard as I can in the nuts. He keels over in pain and tries to run toward his gun on the coffee table. I pull out one of my other knives and throw it right into his back. He drops to the floor and starts crawling to the table. He's a persistent guy. You would think having two knives in you, you would give up the gun. I run over and plunge my other knife into his hand reaching for the gun. It goes through his flesh and the table, pinning his hand in place. He tries to grab it, and I rip the knife in his hand back out and use it to stab his other hand. Both are now pinned to the table. He yells out in pain. I grab a chunk of his hair and punch him in the face.

"That one's for Mary." I hit him again. "That one's for choking me."

His head lolls forward, smacking on the table. He remains motionless now, passed out. Thank god, I was wondering how much pain he could sustain. I'm out of breath. I decide to take a little token to send to Viktor. I was going to just send him a photo, but I think sending him one of Igor's fingers is a much better way to really piss him off.

I place the knife I took out of his shoulder on his finger that wears his Russian Bratva ring, and slice the blade through it, cutting through skin and bone. I look around the room, searching for a cloth, tissue, anything to wrap the finger in. I'm not just gonna put a severed finger in my pocket without anything covering it. My eyes land on a crumpled-up tissue on the floor. This will have to do. I pick it up and wrap Igor's finger in it, and put it in my pocket.

I survey my handywork, Igor's living room now covered in blood. He's not dead yet; I'm going to let him bleed out, and if he happens to wake up and somehow make it to the hospital, his hands will be useless for a long time. Maybe even forever. I definitely damaged the nerves in his hands. He will never hurt Mary or any other woman again. Blood starts to drip down the sides of the table onto the floor. Perfect time for me to leave before I get blood on my shoes standing here.

I reach over him and grab the handles of each knife. "Sorry, Igor, I'm gonna need these back, they're my good knives."

I pull them out of his hand, and his body falls to the ground. I wipe the blood off the blades on Igor's pants and place them back in their sheathes, and exit his house. I get in Maison's car.

"How'd it go?" he asks. "You need me to call a cleanup crew?"

"No need, I didn't kill him. I left him in worse shape than he left his woman, though," I say, smiling, and feeling pretty satisfied with myself.

"Damn."

"But we do have two more stops to make," I tell him.

"Okay, where?" he asks.

"First stop, the nearest gift shop that's still open. I have a little gift I would like to wrap for Viktor," I reply, holding up the severed finger to show him.

He scrunches up his face. "Gnarly, you gonna put a pretty bow on it, too?"

"You know, that's a great idea!"

He smiles. "I do have those from time to time."

CHAPTER 9

Ask and You Shall Receive

Viktor

YESTERDAY WAS A shitshow. Three crates full of weapons were stolen from one of my warehouses by a cartel gang. They usually steal from the Italians, but they must have gotten bored with them and figured they would steal from us instead. No one steals from me; I will rip every last one of those Mexicans' hands off and shove them down each of their throats. Because I was dealing with the mess they left me, and the men they killed, I didn't have time to talk with Igor.

Instead, Violet felt the need to do it herself and dropped off Igor's severed finger to one of the men at my club, in a box with a white bow on top. I know she did it to aggravate me and show me she could finish what I was supposed to—and it did. Not because she killed one of my men without my permission, but she thinks I failed her and put off killing Igor on purpose. And that annoys me. I always keep my word, and don't like her thinking differently of me. Anyone else I wouldn't give a shit what they think, but when it comes to Violet, I do. I open my phone and send her a text.

Thanks for the gift.

Her response comes through almost immediately.

Fuck you.

Clearly, she is still angry with me about Igor.

I take it you're still mad, but seeing as I'm the one currently staring at a box with one of my men's severed fingers inside, I think I should be the mad one, no?

She doesn't respond right away like the last message; in fact, she doesn't respond at all. She apparently wants to be a brat about things. Well, if she won't talk to me, I'll make her. Marco doesn't know she showed up at my club demanding I kill Igor, so I'm guessing he also doesn't know she went against our rules and put him in the hospital. I think a visit to Marco should clear things up and show Violet I'm not to be fucked with. I may want the woman, but I would be a fool to let her think she can attack one of my men and get away with it. I'm going to request a meeting with Marco; we can discuss Violet and the cartel. I pick up the phone and dial his number. It rings a few times before he finally answers.

"Cia, Viktor, what is the problem?"

"You're assuming I have a problem?" I ask.

"Well, we have no business to discuss, and we aren't friends, so the only reason for your call must be you have an issue with something. So, what is it?"

He's right. Marco and I may be at peace with one another, but I wouldn't call us allies.

"It's Violet. She has brutally injured one of my men, and as you know, that goes against our peace treaty. We need to have a meeting to discuss what I would like in return for this inconvenience."

Marco sighs. "Well, it couldn't have come at a better time. I'm in New York for the next few weeks; we can talk at my office tonight at 7:30."

"I will be there," I said.

"I'll make sure my men are aware of your arrival."

He's saying that to ensure I don't get shot by his men for entering his office without a proper appointment. I have to do the same with mine when I host my own meetings. My men are trained to shoot anyone that enters my office unannounced. Well, except for Violet. Whenever she shows up at my club, they know to watch for her, but if any of them put their hands on her, they also know I will kill them with my bare hands. The only man that will be dealing with Violet will be me.

I thank Marco and hang up. Relaxing back in my chair, I open the messages between Violet and me—still no answer from her. She likes to push my buttons, clearly. I may not condone acts of violence against women, but that doesn't mean I don't plan on punishing her the next time I see her. With my phone still in hand, I open an image of Violet entering my club, one I took a screenshot of from my security footage the night we first met. I stare at it, admiring what little I can make out of her face. *You should have never entered my club, little Violet. You've ignited a hunger in me, one I can't seem to sate without you.*

I've gone back and looked at this photo of her a few times today. Is that a bit obsessive? Maybe. But I don't really give a shit. I want her. Crave her. Why? I haven't figured it out yet. She's fueled this desire in me, just from one meeting. From the moment we met, I've only craved more of her, and that's a dangerous thing for a man like me to feel for a woman like her. *Pust' d'yavol budet so mnoy pomyagche v etom voprose.* May the devil go easy on me with this one.

I ARRIVE AT Marco's office, two minutes before 7:30. His New York office is across the street from one of his casinos in a tall glass building. If I'm not mistaken, his wife has an office in this building as well. I start to think about what it would be like to have someone I care for work closely with me. My father's home office was across from my mother's sewing room. He had it that way so he could watch her sew while he worked. And used to say seeing my mother's face when he was stressed about work calmed him. I never touch his office, or hers; I've kept them both the exact same way for years, not wanting to ruin that memory.

I enter the lobby of the building. Two of Marco's men approach me. I tell them my name and they pat me down, telling me to remove my weapons. This is standard protocol for meetings as it keeps both parties safe. My men know I'm here should anything happen to me, so I didn't bother bringing any. Marco and I have both kept our word regarding the peace treaty, so there's no need for extra backup.

Once the pat down is done, his men escort me to Marco's office. It's very dark and similar in size to my office at the club. Its black interior with orange lighting makes it look almost gothic; not the kind of office I expected the Don of the Berlusconi Mafia to have. When we had our peace treaty meeting, it was at my club. We haven't seen each other in person since then. Marco is sitting at his desk, studying some documents on it, and he looks up as I enter.

"Viktor, nice to see you, please sit," he says, gesturing to one of the chairs in front of his desk. I take a seat in the one closest to the door. "Would you like a drink?" he asks.

"No, thank you, I can't stay for long."

He nods in understanding. "I have not spoken to Violet yet, but I have heard from one of the women she works with. It's my understanding that your man, Igor, put this Mary woman in the hospital after you told Violet you would take care of him, correct?"

"Da."

"So you see, Violet had no choice; if she did not act quickly with Igor, Mary would be dead right now."

"I understand her reasoning for going after Igor; that's not the problem. The problem is, I texted her explaining I would take care of it and informed her there would be delays. I had a family matter that was more important at the time, and being a family man yourself, I think you will understand."

"Of course, I understand you had a few minor setbacks, and Violet should have informed me first about everything. I will have a talk with her, but I am not going to punish her for doing what she thought was the right move at the time, so if you're looking for a finger in return from her, you will be sorely disappointed."

It angers me that he would suggest that was something I wanted. I've never portrayed myself as a vile man toward women—men, yes, but never women.

I try to keep my expression neutral. "She can keep her fingers. I'm not interested in harming her as punishment. All I want is a favor."

"Fine, we can agree on that. You let me know when you want to cash it in, and I will do whatever it is you ask."

"Not from you—from Violet. The favor needs to be from her."

Marco now looks uneasy. "I'm not sure Violet will agree to this."

"Well make her agree, then. I am willing to move past this little mishap of hers, if in return, she does a favor for me when I ask."

"Fine, as long as you can promise me this favor will not endanger her in any way, or make her uncomfortable. If it does, then she is allowed to decline. Agreed?"

I nod. "Agreed."

"Great, now that's settled, is there anything else we need to discuss?" he asks.

"Actually, there is one more thing; have you been having trouble with the cartel more than usual lately?"

He considers for a moment. "No, things have been pretty quiet with them now you mention it."

"I figured. One of my shipments was stolen two nights ago by a cartel gang."

"You sure they were part of the cartel?" Marco furrows his brows.

"Da, two of my men that survived the attack saw cartel symbol tattoos on their wrists."

"Hmm, it seems they are now a problem for us both."

"I was thinking it may be beneficial to us both if we worked together to take them down. I can send you whatever my men have uncovered about the gang, and if you have any information as well, I would appreciate it."

He nods. "I will see what I have found and send it your way."

"Thank you, Marco."

"And I hope your family is okay." He adds.

"Yes, my mother was in the hospital, but she is recovering well."

"Good." He says.

We both stand and shake hands. I leave Marco's office and head back to my car, grabbing my gun from his men. I put it in my suit holster on my way out, but before I get to the door, it opens, and Violet walks in. She's stunned to see me at first, then quickly morphs her features into anger. Her dark, feminine energy pours off her, surrounding us both.

"What the fuck are you doing here?" she asks, clearly pissed off.

Her eyes squint a little when she's angry—it's cute. Though I'd *never* tell her that; I wouldn't want to lose one of my own fingers. I haven't seen her since that night at my club, the night my hunger for her started. Now she's here in front of me, and I need to remind myself we are in Marco's building, not my club.

"I was having a meeting with Marco, you know, filling him in on you attacking one of my men without my permission."

"Why didn't you contact me to have a discussion?" she snaps, furious.

"It never crossed my mind to have a meeting with you."

I'm lying, of course. The thought had crossed my mind, but if I spoke with Violet first, we wouldn't get anywhere. She would shut me down about my favor before I even got the chance to tell her what I wanted.

"So what... You thought ratting me out to my brothers was the best choice?"

"Brother, not brothers. Dante was not present, and if you recall, I did try to reach out to you personally, but instead, you thought it was best to send me Igor's finger in a box."

I get closer to her, breathing in her scent. She always smells like fucking fruit; it's both nauseating and intoxicating at the same time.

"That was to show you that you don't lie to me and get away with it." She smiles, clearly pleased with herself.

"I didn't lie to you, Violet, I—"

I stop mid-sentence when I catch a glimpse of fingertip-shaped bruises on her neck. On instinct, I move to brush her hair out of the way so I can get a better look at them.

Violet flinches back from my touch. "What the hell are you doing?" she snaps. She looks both angry and confused as to why I would try to touch her.

I drop my hand back at my side. "Those bruises weren't there when I saw you last."

"How the hell do you know? Were you studying my neck then?"

Yes. I was studying every inch of you, Violet. I don't say it out loud; now is not the time. I need to know what caused those bruises. Better yet, *who* caused them.

"Just answer the damn question, Violet," I demand.

She crosses her arms, glaring daggers at me. "You have your good pal Igor to thank for that. Fucker got me when I was distracted. I never get distracted."

She says the last part quietly, sounding frustrated with herself. Rage consumes me at the thought of Igor putting his hands around her neck. That podonok shouldn't have been anywhere near Violet, and I can't help but feel responsible for that. I'm curious how she got distracted, though. Violet has killed many men, so she's obviously trained to fight well. What could have thrown her off course and given Igor the upper hand?

"What distracted you?" I press.

"What?" Violet asks, taken back by my question.

"If you say you never get distracted, then what caused you to be?"

Violet looks away for a second, momentarily breaking our eye contact. She's hiding something.

"Look, I have more important matters to attend to than to stand here and answer your stupid questions."

"Stupid?" I raise a brow.

"Yes."

She brushes past me but stops halfway, turning back to me. "Oh, and by the way, don't *ever* get Marco and Dante involved in our business again."

She walks away before I get the chance to ask her "Or what?" *What will you do, little redhead?* My mind conjures up a hundred ways that conversation could have gone if I had said those words to her. Us bickering back and forth, her threatening to kill me or cut off my cock, my cock ending up in her mouth instead. Yes, I definitely like that last scenario a whole lot better. Ignoring my lustful thoughts of Violet for now, I leave Marco's building. I also have more important matters to attend to. Like checking in on poor Igor at the hospital.

I ARRIVE AT the hospital Igor's been admitted to and go to his room. Sergio is standing guard outside, and he nods in respect before opening the door for me. Igor is sitting up in his bed, both his hands wrapped in gauze along with his shoulder. His face is purple with bruises; she fucked him up pretty bad. *Good girl.*

"Privet, Igor', ty vyglyadish' v plokhom sostoyanii." *Hi, Igor, you look in bad shape.*

"Net, spasibo etoy ryzhey suchke." *No thanks to that red-haired bitch.*

I clench my fists and hold them at my sides, not ready to unleash my anger on him yet.

I approach his bed, standing near his heart monitor. "No ty pokazal yey, kto zdes' glavnyy, verno." *But you showed her who's boss, right?*

"Ya pochti ubil etu suchku, i kak tol'ko ya popravlyus', ya zakonchu rabotu." *I almost killed that bitch, and as soon as I get better, I'll finish the job.* His tone is full of pride. I unplug his heart monitor.

"Chto ty delayesh', boss?" *What are you doing, boss?* His expression is now one of concern. I lunge for him and wrap both my hands around his throat.

"Pakhan," he chokes out.

I squeeze until he can no longer speak; his eyes are wide with a mix of fear and confusion. Good. I want him to feel what Violet felt when he choked her, and how Mary must have felt every time he hit her. Igor's face starts turning blue. I remove a hand from his throat, and he sucks in a breath. He thinks I'm done with him, letting him live, and that's exactly what I want him to think. One hand still on his throat, I move it up to grip his jaw and move my other hand to the back of his head.

I look him dead in the eyes, letting him see the darkness in mine. "Ty bol'she nikogda ne podnimesh' ruku na Moyu Vayolet ili na lyubuyu druguyu zhenshchinu." *You will never lay a hand on my Violet, or any women, again.*

With a vicious twist of his head, his neck snaps. I leave him in the hospital bed and leave the room. Sergio follows behind me. I will let Igor be a lesson to my men, to all men, that Violet Berlusconi is mine—and you don't touch what's mine.

CHAPTER 10

Filthy

Violet

I BARELY GOT any sleep last night, unable to believe that asshole actually went to Marco before I could. Viktor did it on purpose; he wanted to get a rise out of me. I spoke with Marco after my altercation with Viktor, and he told me all about Viktor's favor he expects from me. When I tried to fight Marco on it, he reminded me that "Those stupid favors saved your life once." And he's right, but that doesn't mean the whole thing isn't fucking ridiculous. What could Viktor possibly want from me? He probably only wants the favor as part of some sick game he's playing.

To be honest, I didn't think he cared this much about Igor. When I first spoke to him, he seemed like he had no problem exterminating him. Yet, when I saw him last night, his feelings had changed. He looked angry when I mentioned the bruising on my neck was from Igor, and that I stabbed him for it. His whole demeanor changed then; he seemed amused by our arguing before, but when I stormed off, he looked like he wanted to stab me in the back like I did to Igor.

My phone vibrates on my desk. I pick it up and open my messages—speak of the devil. Viktor's number pops up with a text from him. I saved his name under Russian Asshole, because why not?

> **I would like to cash in my favor.**

That's all his text says.

> Wow, that was fast, fuck something up already?

No , I just don't like to waste time.

Waste time over what? What could he need done so fast that he's willing to cash in this favor already?

> Whatever, what's the favor?

You will find out tonight.

What the fuck is his problem? Why can't he tell me over text? Our line is safe; if he needed me to kill someone for him, he could just say.

> Why can't you tell me now? If this is some sort of game, I'm not interested.

He's just trying to fuck with me, probably gets off on making women miserable.

I do not play games, Violet. Tonight, end of discussion. Be at the club for 10:30, my men will direct you to my office.

I send him a middle finger emoji.

Viktor doesn't respond to my last text. That man infuriates me like no other. I'm used to men pissing me off, but Viktor gets so under my skin, I want to rip it off. Unfortunately, there's no choice but to go to his club tonight. Marco will never let me live it down if I don't, and I'm worried Viktor will cause real issues for Marco if I don't.

I text Maison to see if he will give me a lift. I don't like taking my car, because I don't trust Marco's—and my—enemies here not to tamper with it. The last time I drove myself to an event, someone must have been watching me, because when I went back down to the underground parking lot, the security guard was passed out, and my car had *Mafia Slut* spray-painted all over it. Of course, I found the men who did it and killed them, but if I can avoid another situation like that, I will. My phone dings, distracting me from my thoughts. It's Maison.

> Hey, buttercup, I would love to give you a ride tonight, but I went out last night and have been in the bathroom all day, if you know what I mean. Brought a super hot girl home though, so it was worth it ;) Can you get one of Marco's drivers to take you?

I roll my eyes at the nickname. Maison always has some stupid nickname he comes up with. He does it to annoy me, and yes, we have a friendly relationship, but he forgets that I am also his boss.

> Yes I can. Call me buttercup again, and you will no longer be working for me.

> Sorry, boss, won't happen again.

I met Maison through Marco. His mother was kidnapped and trafficked by the cartel, and Marco found her. But he was too late; they had killed her. Maison's father left when he was a baby, so it was just him and his mother. Until it was just him. He was only fourteen, a kid, and went to the police about his mother's disappearance. Told them men broke into their house and kidnapped her. They didn't believe him, though. She had drugs in the house when they searched the place. They assumed she was a junky and ran off like his father did. Poor Maison was in foster care after that, but because of his age and family history, no one wanted him.

So Maison ran away, and ended up living on the streets of New York. Marco tracked down some of the families of the women that were killed that night. He wanted to give them closure and help them out any way he could. He found Maison on the street one day, beating the shit out of some guys that were trying to steal a lady's purse. Marco saw something in him then, similar to what he must have seen in me, and instead of just offering him money, he offered Maison a chance at a new life. Because we shared similar childhood trauma, I have more of a connection with Maison than any of Marco's other men, so when Marco asked me who I wanted for my assistant, I chose Maison. He can be a real pain in my ass at times, but I couldn't imagine working with any other man.

It's 9:30 p.m. I really should be getting ready for my meeting with Viktor. I open my closet and pick an outfit to wear, deciding on a satin mini skirt, nylons and a sheer blouse with my favorite heel boots. If I plan on fighting with Viktor about this stupid favor of his, I'm going to look hot doing it.

I ARRIVE AT Viktor's club at 11:00 instead of 10:30 because fuck him. I'm not his pet; I don't respond to his demands. At the back entrance, the same meathead as last time guards the door. He looks me up and down then opens the door for me. Two guards welcome me inside and take me to see Viktor.

When I first came to his club, his men looked ready to kill me at any given chance, but now, they don't even glance in my direction, like they're afraid to look at me. Strange—maybe word got out about what I did to Igor, and Viktor's men are afraid I'll do the same to them.

We reach Viktor's office, and I step inside. It has the same red lighting as the rest of the club, but it doesn't look as tacky in here. Viktor is sitting behind his desk, his attention solely on me as I enter.

"You're late." He states the obvious.

"My life doesn't revolve around your schedule, Viktor. I'm here, so what's this favor you need?" I ask.

He moves from behind his desk and leans against it, crossing his arms. He's dressed more casually today. His muscular arms are bare in a black T-shirt, matched with black cargo pants and instead of black leather dress shoes, he's wearing black combat boots. When I saw him last, he had the whole rugged-older-dominant-businessman look going on, but now, Viktor looks like he's ready to go to war, and I suddenly feel underdressed for this meeting.

I catch Viktor's eyes glancing at my legs; they linger there for a few minutes, longer than they should. Never mind, I wore just the right thing. I'm trying hard not to look at his biceps. When his arms are crossed, it makes them look even bigger. He has a few tattoos on his arms, but he's not covered in ink like Marco and Dante. Most of them look to be Russian symbols and words, which in a strange way makes them look more dangerous, and not knowing what they mean... I subtly cross my legs a bit, feeling wetness between them.

Come on, Violet, get it the fuck together. We hate this man, remember?

"I want you to have dinner with me," he says bluntly. All sexual thoughts disappear from my brain at Viktor's words.

"Dinner? You gotta be fucking kidding me! I knew this was going to be a waste of my time, why on earth would I go to dinner with you?" I shout, pissed the hell off.

"It's what I want," he says casually, as if asking me to dinner is not a big deal.

"Why?" I scrunch my nose. He has to be joking. There's no way a man like him would only want dinner as his favor.

"Why not?" he replies.

"Stop with the vague answers, you could ask for anything, me to kill someone for you, anything!"

"I have men for that," he states.

"You could even get me to do your dishes for you, clean your house, and I couldn't say no, but you choose dinner!"

"While the idea of you on your hands and knees cleaning my house in a sexy maid's outfit does appeal to me, I already have a maid cleaning my house as we speak. I want to take you to dinner, and that's what I'm going to get." He moves toward me. "We can argue about it all night, but it won't change."

"Well I rather wash your fucking dishes than go to dinner with you," I snap.

Viktor and I are so close now that if I were to take one step forward, our noses would be touching.

His deep brown eyes bore into mine. "You are testing my patience," he says quietly, tone laced with irritation.

"Good. I'm not going to dinner with you, Viktor. Either pick something else, or you can shove your favor up your ass!"

He grabs my jaws. "How about I shove my cock down your throat instead, hm? Make you get on your knees right now and empty my balls as your favor, would you rather that?" he growls.

The lust in his eyes is clear. Anger stirs within me; how dare he think he can say that shit to me, and why the fuck am I getting turned on by it? I can picture myself doing just that, on this office floor. I need to push back, change the subject, something. The tension in the room grows by the second.

"You can try, but you won't have them by the end," I say with a smile.

"I've tried to be nice and respectful to you, but your bratty little mouth keeps making it hard, too; perhaps you need a lesson in respect. The old

Russian way," he smolders.

"And what's that, exactly? Beating women into submission? How is dear Igor, anyway?" I ask, curious. Not that I really give a shit.

"Dead. I killed him, don't change the subject," he says firmly.

I arch a brow, confused. "Why did you kill him? I fucked him up pretty bad, and Mary is long gone by now."

"I didn't kill him for her. I killed him because he put his hands around your fucking neck where only mine belong!" Rage flows through him like lava.

"Yours don't belong there, either, and if you touch me again, I'll put a knife through your hand like I did Igor's."

Viktor grabs my throat—not hard, but enough to piss me off.

"Stop saying his name before you make me more angry."

Me? How the fuck is he the one mad when his hand is around my neck? Fuck him! I reach for my knife in my thigh sheath and slash it through Viktor's bicep, cutting him deep. He looks at the gash in his arm and then back to me. He didn't even flinch and is showing no signs of pain. Instead, there's lust and darkness in his eyes again.

Fuck. Well that backfired.

"You shouldn't have done that, malyshka," he says with a grin, the Russian pet name throwing me off.

He grabs me so fast and with such strength, I'm thrown over his desk before I even know what's happening. His hand is pinning me to the desk, and I fight him, kicking and grabbing things to try and throw behind me at him. I try to headbutt him with the back of my skull, but he moves before my head connects with his.

"Nice try," he growls.

"Get the fuck off me, Viktor ! I swear to god I'll kill you!"

"I doubt you believe in God, Violet, but you will once I'm done with you." He pulls my skirt up around my hips, exposing my ass to him.

"Viktor!" I yell. "What the fuck are you do—"

My words are cut off by the *smack* he just landed on my right ass cheek. A stinging sensation starts to bloom on that spot. *This motherfucker just spanked me!* His hand lifts and he spanks my other cheek. He does it again and again, a moan slipping free from my lips, and I'm secretly hoping he doesn't hear it. I can't give him the satisfaction of knowing that I like to be spanked. It's been a kink of mine since I was a teen, but all my previous boyfriends never liked doing it. My last boyfriend did, but he sucked at it; he never smacked hard enough or just wasn't into it.

Viktor, on the other hand, knows exactly how to spank me, and the fact that he's doing it to punish me makes it even hotter. Wetness slides down my thighs and into my nylons. Viktor stops spanking me. He shifts his feet back a bit.

"You like it when I spank you, don't you, Violet?" he rasps.

Fuck, he noticed how wet I am. *Deny it! Deny it, Violet, don't let him know how much he is affecting you,* I think to myself.

"No! Fuck you!"

Smack! He spanks me again.

"Bad girl! Try again."

I breathe heavily; his last spank was harder than the others. "Okay, I'll admit that... that I'm going to enjoy killing you after this!"

He makes a deep, annoyed groaning sound in response, and kicks my legs open, spreading my legs and forcing my back to arch over his desk even more. *Smack*! Viktor lands a spank right on my fucking pussy. I cry out in both pleasure and pain, the slap landing right over my clit. A burning, tingling sensation forms all over my pussy. Viktor's hand moves from my back, no longer keeping me pinned to the desk, yet I don't move. I could kick him in the balls right now and run out that door. But I don't. I stay planted right to his desk. Why? I'm afraid of that answer. I turn my head slightly on the desk to see what he's doing. Viktor is on his haunches, staring at my ass.

"Fuck, this perfect ass," he groans.

He rips my nylons with his bare hands, tearing them and my thong, too. He spreads my ass cheeks apart, exposing my bare pussy to him. He blows a gentle breath. Fuck, I'm so turned on, that little breath of air feels amazing. I moan and Viktor bites my left ass cheek, his teeth sinking deep into my skin. He does the same to the other one, and I cry out from the sting of the bite, the pain morphing into pleasure. Call me a sadist all you want, but I enjoy pain with pleasure; a lot of people do, and I think Viktor's just discovered that. He blows on my pussy again.

"Viktor, please," I beg.

What am I begging for? For him to stop or keep going? I don't even know anymore.

"Are you begging me to stop, Violet? Or do you want more?" he asks in a sensual tone.

"I—I don't know."

Only I *do* know, and as much as I don't want to admit it to myself, my pussy craves Viktor's touch.

"Hmm, let's find out."

Viktor's tongue licks lazily at my clit, teasing the sensitive bundle of nerves. I moan with each lick he gives me. He presses harder on my clit with his tongue then begins to suck on it. My moans grow louder throughout his office, and I'm thankful for the loud music outside so no one can hear me. Viktor spanks my ass while sucking on my clit, and one of his fingers circles my entrance; he slips his thick finger inside me and starts fucking me with it. He moans into my pussy, and it's the hottest fucking sound I've ever heard. Tension rises in my stomach. Viktor slaps my ass one more time and removes his mouth and finger from my pussy.

"I need more of you," he says, standing.

He flips me over on the desk so my back is laying on it, then he lifts both my legs and places them on the desk, too. My legs automatically spread open for him. He steps between them and reaches for my blouse, grabbing a fistful of the fabric. He shreds it in two, leaving only scraps behind. My breasts are still covered by my lace bra.

Viktor stares at my body, admiring it. "Telo etoy zhenshchiny bylo sozdano dlya togo, chtoby ya yemu poklonyalsya." *This woman's body was created for me to worship.*

He says something in Russian that I don't understand. Viktor grabs the cups of my bra and pulls them down, exposing my breasts. They're not overly big; mine are more medium to small size. I used to hate them, but by Viktor's hungry expression, he clearly doesn't.

He takes one of my nipples into his mouth, sucking and biting on it. *Jesus, I could come just from him doing that.* He does the same to the other, alternating between sucking and biting. He kisses his way down my chest, taking little nips at my skin along the way. When he gets to my spread thighs, he bites each one and kisses where he bit, soothing it. Each bite feels like he's marking me, like he wants me to have these marks for days so I can remember this night. His face is so close to my pussy, I can't take it anymore. I need him there again, I need to come. Viktor must sense my urgency, because he does just that. His mouth wraps around my clit, sucking the hell out of it.

"Chert voz'mi, u tebya khoroshiy vkus."

"English, please," I say breathlessly.

"I said, fuck, you taste good, I could eat this perfect little pussy all night."

God this man really knows the right things to say. Viktor continues to suck on my clit, and two of his thick fingers penetrate me. He fucks me with his fingers while he feasts on my clit. I'm getting closer and closer to coming, and my body tenses, begging for release. As I'm about to climax, Viktor stops sucking. His fingers are still inside me, but they're still.

"Why did you stop?" I ask him, frustrated.

"Look at this slutty little pussy, so eager to come for me," he growls.

"Yes, please, I was about to—"

"Oh, I know you were, Violet, but you don't deserve to come, not after the way you spoke to me." He removes his fingers and stands up. *Is he fucking serious right now?*

"Viktor, please!" I beg.

He rubs my spread thighs. "You beg so beautifully, Violet, but you still don't deserve to come yet."

"Fuck you!" I yell.

He smacks my pussy again, the tip of his fingers connecting with my clit and the flat of his palm hitting the rest. I cry out, my pussy becoming more and more sensitive the longer I'm refused my release.

"If you say yes to dinner, you can come," he says.

"Fuck, fine! Whatever you want, Viktor. I don't care, just please, for the love of god, make me come!" I'm desperate now.

Viktor smirks down at me. He unbuckles his belt, the metal clinging together as he does. His arm is still dripping blood down his bicep, but he doesn't pay any attention to it. He unzips and takes his cock out. I can't see it properly in this lighting or at this angle, but I have no doubt it's as hot as the rest of him. *Is he going to fuck me? Do I want him to?* Viktor rubs the head of his cock over my clit, and the sensation is like nothing I've ever felt before. His cock feels like velvet rubbing against my pussy, smooth and soft. I want him inside me—*need* him inside me.

Viktor moans, "Do you want my cock, malyshka?"

"Yes," I moan. Who the hell am I? I don't beg men for anything; why do I do it so easily for him? It's like I've stepped out of my own mind and body and into someone else's. He rubs his cock faster on my clit, and the tension builds in my stomach again.

"That's it, Violet, come for me."

I do as he says. My body releases all the tension I've been holding, my vision blurs and I scream my release out into his office. Minutes later, I'm still tingling from head to toe and feeling slightly high; I came so hard, I thought I was going to black out. I lazily look up at Viktor. He looks like a Russian god, and from the way he's looking back at me, he's clearly not done with me yet.

Viktor slowly slides his hard, thick cock over my wet pussy, down to my entrance. He circles it, teasing me. Just when I think he's about to plunge into me, he backs away.

"I wish I could give you my cock, Violet, but you don't deserve it yet. I made you come, but that's all you get. Maybe next time you'll choose your words more wisely. That being said, watching you come has made my cock hard as steel, so instead of fucking you, I'm going to jerk myself off, make you watch and paint this beautiful body of yours in my cum."

My pussy clenches at his words. I watch him move his hand up and down his length, the veins in his arms bulging from how tight he's gripping it. God, it's hot as fuck. I'm getting more turned on by the sight of him getting himself off. Viktor pumps his cock faster, grunting in pleasure. I don't know what comes over me, but this overwhelming need takes over to see him come and feel it on my body. I spread my legs further apart for him and give him a needy, seductive look.

"Fuck!" is all he shouts just before he comes, warm ropes of white landing on my stomach and chest. Both of us are now panting from pleasure. I look into Viktor's eyes, the sexual haze now dissipating. Viktor puts his cock back inside his pants and zips them up. He leaves me laying there on his desk, his cum still on my skin. Fucking asshole. I can't say I expected anything else.

I sit up, trickles of his release sliding down my body when I move. I look around the desk for a tissue or something, when a door opens at the other end of the office and Viktor comes back holding a hand towel. *Oh, so that's where he went.* I thought that room was a closet, but it must be a washroom. He approaches me and I reach out to him to give me the cloth. He pulls it away, and I give him a confused look.

"Lay down," he orders.

I lay back down on his desk and Viktor runs the cloth over my stomach; it's wet but warm as he circles it up to my chest, cleaning himself off me. Once he's done, I sit up again, then he tosses the cloth in the trashcan next to his desk and I hop off it. I bend down to reach for my skirt and put it back on, then search for my discarded blouse when I remember Viktor shredded it. He finds it and picks it up, inspecting his handy work. He throws it in the trash with the cloth and starts taking his T-shirt off. I can't help but ogle at his body. He hands me the shirt and I take it, since I don't really have any other option unless I want to walk through a club full of people and Russian mafia men in my lace bra. I put the shirt on and am immediately hit by his warm, spicy scent.

"Thank you," I say to him.

He nods. Well, this is awkward. I can't believe I let him do those things to me. I haven't let a man touch me in years, and I just let Viktor do things to me that I have fantasized about since I was nineteen. And I begged him for it. I need to get the fuck out of this office. Viktor is probably itching to brag to his men about what he did to me. Without saying a word, I grab the handle of his office door, ready to leave.

"Violet." Viktor calls my name as I open the door.

I look over my shoulder at him. "What?" I snap back.

"I will be collecting that favor soon," he says, his voice low.

I give him a dirty look and storm out as fast as I can. I never want to step foot in this fucking club again. What happened tonight was a mistake, a stupid mistake fueled by lust and built-up sexual frustration, that's it! Viktor will never touch me again, and if he tries... I. Will. Kill. Him. Even if it starts a war between the Russians and the Italians. I'll go to dinner with him, then my life will go back to being Viktor-free as though we never met.

CHAPTER 11

Sem'ya

Family

Viktor

FRIDAY NIGHTS ARE my cooking nights with Mama. We haven't done one since she got back from the hospital, but since she has been doing better, she asked if I could come over and cook pelmeni with her. I've spent the last few nights hunting cartel members to find the bastards who stole from me, and I could use a break—that and a much needed distraction from Violet.

Images of her, laid out on my desk for me, have been plaguing my mind since I got home last night. It took more strength than you can imagine to let her leave my office without fucking her. The way she begged me, I was ready to give her anything she asked me for. She could have asked me to eat her pussy until I passed out, and I would have gladly done it. She looked so beautiful, with my cum on her skin. I should have let her sit there, waited until it dried and seeped into her skin, marking her. I wonder how fast it took her to rip my shirt off and burn it once she got home.

Alexie, one of my men, had to stitch the wound she gave me, which now acts as another constant reminder of her. One that will scar me forever. It's a shame I didn't give her one in return. Maybe not a permanent one, but I left my mark on almost every inch of her body. Every bite, every suck, and every lick will remind Violet of how she submitted to my every touch. Once I got home, I fucked my hand in the shower because I was so turned on thinking about how I made her come. I needed another release from not being able to fuck her.

She may be in control of her own life, but when it's just her and I, she needs to know I'm the one in control. Violet needs a dominant man in her life, not as a friend or a brother, but a partner. She acted like what we did meant nothing to her, but I could see the truth in her eyes while I was cleaning my cum off her soft skin, and now that I've had a taste of her, she's mine. I just have to try and break through her cold, tough-bitch exterior to make her see that.

I arrive at my mama's house, trying to focus now on her and not Violet. The last thing I need is to get hard in the middle of cooking dinner with my mother. Dimitry has amped up the security and amount of guards here since the cartel gang incident. I'm not taking any risks with those mudaks! *Assholes.* Mama is already in the kitchen when I enter.

"Privet, Mama," I say to her. She has flour poured all over the counter and has begun to roll the dough to form the pelmeni.

"Privet, Viktor, come. I cut the dough, you shape," she orders.

I nod and roll up the sleeves of my dress shirt and get to work, grabbing the pieces of dough Mama has cut and stuffing them with the pork filling.

"So, what's new, my son? You seem more troubled today," she asks.

I can never hide anything from this woman; she sees right through me. Always has since I was a boy. Lying to her or hiding my feelings was never an option. To the rest of the world and my men, I'm an evil Pakhan of the Russian Bratva, but to her, I am still her sweet little boy, despite the monstrous things I have done.

When I was seventeen, I ripped out a classmate's tongue with my bare hands and made his other friend eat it, for talking badly about my family. My father scolded me at first, but when I told him what the boy had called Mama, he went over to the boy's house and did the same to his father. I was taken out of that school and finished my last years of high school at home with tutors. I didn't mind it, because I got to spend my breaks cooking with

Mama and training at home with my father. I've become a more brutal and violent man since taking my father's place, cutting out men's body parts and torturing them. Compared to what I have done, ripping out a man's tongue is more like child's play.

"I am fine, Mama, just dealing with the stolen shipment and finding the ones responsible is taking time."

"Net! That is not why; something else upsets you. I can feel it, do not lie to me, syn."

I sigh, pinching the edges of the dough together to form the dumplings. I can't very well tell her about Violet and how I haven't been able to get the taste of her sweet pussy out of my head and off my tongue. *Yebat! Fuck!* So much for keeping my head clear of her.

"There is this woman that I have become interested in," I admit to her, though 'interested' is an understatement; I've become obsessed with her.

"Ah, that is why. I knew it! Only a woman could make my Viktor lose his mind," she said.

I laugh. "I haven't lost my mind, Mama... Well, not yet."

"So she is a tough woman, then?"

"How did you guess?" I ask.

"The good ones always are. You do not like meek women, Viktor. Much like your father, he did marry me after all," she says, smiling at me. "So what is the problem? You like her, no?" she asks.

"Da."

"And she likes you?"

I have to think about that for a second; she definitely liked what I did to her in my office.

"To be honest, Mama, I'm not sure. She is complicated."

"Most women are. This is nothing, how complicated could one woman be?" she asks with a chuckle.

She is right, but Violet has a darkness in her, one I recognize very well within myself, only hers feels slightly different. I'm drawn to it, and I can't explain why.

"So you try. She will learn to like you . If she is a tough woman, that means she hasn't had an easy life. It will take time to win her heart, Viktor. You just have to decide if it's worth the trouble. You remember how your father and I met?"

How could I forget? Whenever my father would say my mother was annoying him, she would bring up how he wouldn't leave her alone when they first met.

"He came to my work every day, asking me to go out with him, and every time I said no! Until one day, I got so tired of him, I said yes so he would go away!" she says, waving her hand.

My father definitely was a persistent man. When he wanted something, he didn't stop until he got it—whether it was my mama, a shipment, or some other gang's territory, he was ruthless.

"I was a young girl, I studied hard, but I knew what kind of man your father was. I didn't say no to him because I didn't like him. I said it because I was trying to protect my heart. Violet could be doing the same. You don't know what that girl has been through."

She's right, as usual. I don't know, but I want to. I know nothing about her life before joining Marco.

"If your Papa hadn't seen I was worth the fight, we never would have been together. So, you go out with her, and see in your heart if she is worth fighting for."

"Thanks, Mama," I say softly, kissing her cheek.

"You're welcome, moya malen'kaya kapusta."

"Mama, you need to stop calling me that."

"But it makes me smile. You don't want your mother to smile?"

I sigh, shaking my head. "Yes, Mama, of course I do."

"Good, now don't eat too many dumplings. Once they are done, I put cabbage in them, and I don't want you to be gassy for your date."

I sigh again, ignoring her. Tomorrow, I will cash in my favour. The whole dinner might blow up in my face, or end with one of Violet's knives in it.

CHAPTER 12

It's A ~~Man's~~ Woman's World

Violet

MY PHONE RINGS as I put a pot of water on the stove for my pasta. Fridays are pasta nights; it won't be as good as the pasta I eat in Italy when I visit, but I would say mine is a close second. I turn my phone over on the kitchen counter—it's a Facetime call from Sabrina. After answering, the screen switches to Sabrina and Nikki's smiling faces.

"Hey, bitch!" they both yell through the phone. There's loud music playing in the background.

"Where are you guys?" I ask, not able to see what's behind them since both their faces are so close to the camera.

"We're at La Porta Del Cielo!" Nikki yells.

Heaven's Gate—Dante's club. He's owned it for years but has changed a few things since marrying Nikki. It used to be a strip club with trashy women, gambling and fighting. Now, it's become both his and Nikki's club they own together. Strippers have been replaced with professional Burlesque dancers, tasteful women in cages, and no gambling. Well, at least not any Nikki's aware of.

"Come join us! We're having a girls' night while the men stay home." Sabrina laughs.

"I wish I could, but it's pasta night. I'm going to turn on some tunes and relax for the night. This week has been a lot," I tell them, not mentioning *why* it's been a lot.

My confusing-as-fuck feelings for *Viktor.*

"Boo! Lame!" Nikki yells.

She's obviously been drinking already. Nikki doesn't get out much since becoming a mom and is probably wasted after one drink.

I laugh at her. "Okay, well you guys have fun. Bye now!" I wave to the camera.

"Bye! Love you!"

I shake my head at them. "Love you, too."

I hang up and set my phone back on the counter. I turn the stove burner on high to boil my pasta water. My house is in a rural neighborhood in Cold Spring, New York, which is about an hour and fifteen minute drive from New York City. If I'm doing a kill job in New York City or any business for Marco, I usually stay at his penthouse. But on days I have no work, and the girls have nothing they need at the Help Center, I enjoy my peaceful alone time away from the city.

I may have grown up in Toronto, but I was never a fan of big cities, so when I had to move to New York with Marco, I wanted my very own safe haven to escape to. My closest neighbor is at the end of the street, so I'm completely alone up here, which is how I like it. I have a state-of-the-art security system, similar to the one Marco has at his house in Italy, plus some of my own hidden booby traps I've added since buying the place. There's no guards here because there's no need for them; I can protect myself if someone were to find out where I live. I haven't shared my location with anyone—not Marco, not Dante, not even Maison knows where I live. Whenever he and I meet, it's always at Marco's penthouse.

I decide to turn on some music while I cook. "Gimme Gimme" by Abba plays over my surround sound speakers. As I hum to its tune, I chop sun-dried tomatoes for my pasta sauce. Before I toss them in a pan, an alarm for my security system goes off. I go over to my computer and hit the button to open double screens of my back and front yards.

"What the fuck?" I say out loud.

There's four men, all in black tactical gear with guns, hiding out around the forested area of my backyard. *How did you fuckers find me?* One of them creeps out of the woods and starts approaching my home. *I wouldn't do that if I were you, buddy.*

I smile at the screen, knowing he's about to step right on the bear trap that's covered by leaves and other debris. The shallow hole is the same size as the trap, so it can sink into it, hiding it even more. The man runs and his right foot lands in the trap, snapping closed on his leg. His scream is silent because my cameras can't pick up sound that far away, but the agonizing look of pain on his face is blatantly clear. His companions stop in their tracks and scan the surrounding area for any other traps. They won't find them.

The water is boiling on the stove, so I leave my computer, placing the pasta into the pot and stirring it. There's another beep, and I drop the spoon on the counter. It's letting me know that the three other men are getting closer to the house; they have abandoned their friend who is struggling to get the bear trap off his foot. *Good luck with that, asshole.* I laugh at him. I click the screen to zoom in on the man that's about to walk into my next trap. He runs between two trees, but his body is stopped abruptly by the metal wire now slicing through his throat, nearly decapitating him.

And then there were two. A devious smile forms on my face when the last two men duck under the wire and approach the backdoor. Well, they're certainly determined. I wonder who hired them to kill me. They don't appear to be part of the cartel; home invasions aren't exactly their style. It's too planned. I'll have to try to keep one alive to find out.

As I wait for them to enter the house, I turn off all the lights downstairs, only leaving the light from the stove on in the kitchen. I grab the knife on the counter and hide behind the door of my pantry closet. My music is still playing over the speaker, but the faint sound of their footsteps approaching the kitchen still cuts through. Once one of them gets close to the door, I kick it open, and it slams into one of the men's faces.

I throw my kitchen knife at the other one. It lands in the middle of his chest, and his body hits the wooden floor. The last man grabs me from behind and I headbutt him, slamming my elbow into his gut. He manages to push me into the counter, but I turn around quickly, grabbing the boiling pot of water and throwing it right into the man's face. He screams and covers his face as I kick him, knocking him to the ground. I pick up his gun that he dropped, aiming it right at his head.

"Who the fuck hired you?" I shout.

"Fuck you!" he grunts, rolling around on the ground, clenching his teeth in pain. I shoot him in the kneecap, and he howls, grabbing his leg.

"I have no patience tonight. I'm hungry, and you and your friends ruined my dinner plans, so I'm only going to ask this one more time. Who hired you to kill me?"

The man spits at my feet. Okay, patience officially gone, I'll figure it out myself. I aim the gun back at his head and pull the trigger, his head snapping back from the force of the bullet. My kitchen is now covered in blood, pasta, and water. So much for a nice, quiet evening at home. I roll my eyes and step over various puddles of water to get to my phone on the counter, then dial Marco's number.

"Hey, I'm gonna need a cleanup crew. Yeah, I'm fine." He asks me how many I'll need. "One should be fine," I say, almost forgetting about the two men in my backyard. "Actually, make it two."

WHILE WAITING FOR the cleanup crew, I make myself some new pasta. Did I make it while there were still two dead bodies in my kitchen? Yes. I'm hungry and can't wait any longer. The crew arrives and cleans my kitchen while I sit with my bowl of pasta in my living room. My phone rings. *Why is Viktor calling me?* We haven't talked since... Well, since he ate my pussy in his office and made me come harder than I ever have.

When he spoke Russian... Ugh. I expected his accent to be strong, but I guess years of living in America has changed that. I never thought I was the kind of woman that got turned on from a man's voice. Usually when men speak, it makes me wanna die, or make them die, not make me wet. But Viktor's voice seems to do the trick. He shouldn't be allowed to speak with a voice like that. Next time, maybe I'll slash his tongue. *Next time? There will be no next time, get it together, Violet.*

I decline the call and continue eating my pasta. I really don't have the energy for him tonight, and am still feeling slightly awkward and pissed off from what happened. I finally stopped thinking about him, only to be reminded again. He calls a second time.

Oh, for fuck's sake. "What?!" I answer.

"You should work on your greetings," he says, his deep voice sending a tingle down my spine.

"What do you want, Viktor? I'm busy."

"I'm cashing in my favor. Tomorrow night, 7:00. Wear a nice dress. I'll pick you up at your place."

"You don't know where I live!" I tell him.

"I have ways of finding things out, Violet."

"Wait, are you the one who sent those men to my house?!"

"What men?" he asks, sounding genuinely confused.

"Never mind," I say nervously.

No, it couldn't have been Viktor. If he wanted me dead, he had ample opportunity to do so while we were in his office.

"I was talking about Marco's penthouse."

"Oh, right, fine. I'll be ready, but once this dinner is over and the favor has been fulfilled, you and I are done!"

"Whatever you say, Violet," he says sarcastically.

"I mean it, Viktor!"

"7 p.m. Don't be late, or I'll be forced to come up and drag you down myself."

He hangs up before I get to say "Fuck you." I pick up the bowl of pasta, which is no longer appetizing and toss it in the garbage. I meant what I said; once this dinner is over, I'm blocking Viktor's number, and if he tries to contact me or show back up in my life, I'll make his a living fucking hell.

CHAPTER 13
The Devil Has Red Hair

Viktor

I WAIT OUTSIDE Marco's penthouse for Violet, right at 7:00 p.m., leaning against my black Hellcat. She's late again. I wasn't bluffing when I told her I would come up and get her if she wasn't down here on time. I left the part out about me spanking her for making me wait. The building's front doors finally open and Violet walks out. I didn't know a man like me could have my breath taken away so easily. Violet looks like sin in an emerald-green satin dress that clings to her body in the most perfect way. She walks toward me like a siren, beckoning me from the depths of hell, and I will gladly go down there with her.

Her heels click on the concrete. She's an inch taller in them, making her almost 5 '2 and her hair's done up, with red waves cascading down her fair-skinned shoulders. All I can think about is wrapping those luscious waves around my fist and pulling her head back while I take her from behind. Jesus Christ, I need to get it together before I get hard and take her right here in front of Marco's building.

"Viktor," she greets me. "Let's get this over with."

She moves past me to open the passenger door. For a woman with such soft facial features, she can sharpen them quickly.

I reach my hand out in front of her to stop her. "Let me get it," I offer.

"There's no need to play the gentleman, Viktor, this isn't a real date."

I step closer to her, getting right in her face. "Such a mouthy little brat you are, malyshka."

"Don't call me that! I might not know Russian, but I've been around enough Russian men with Marco to know what that means. I'm not your fucking baby girl."

She can say that all she likes, but the way her body flushed when I called her that in my office tells me otherwise. I open the door for her despite her protest. She doesn't thank me when she climbs in, and I would expect nothing less from her. I shut the passenger door and walk around to the driver's side and climb in.

"Nice car," she says.

"Wow, a compliment."

"Don't let it go to your head."

I clench my jaw. This is going to be a long night if she's getting me wound up already. "Speaking of compliments, you look beautiful, Violet," I say, causing her to blush.

She turns her head away from me to look out the window. "Thank you." I smirk and start the car. "So, where are we going?" she asks. "And please don't say a Russian restaurant to eat borscht," she adds in a disgusted tone.

"No, we are going to a Greek restaurant. You like Greek food, don't you?" I ask.

"Yeah, how did you know that?" She eyes me suspiciously.

"I didn't, you just told me, so that is where we are going."

She rolls her eyes. "I'm surprised you didn't have your favor more planned out."

"Well, it's a little hard to plan when you won't tell me anything about yourself. It's like pulling teeth with you."

"I'd rather be pulling out someone's teeth than be here with you," she says under her breath.

My jaw clenches again, and I focus on the road. I place my right hand on her bare thigh, gripping it slightly. Her chest rises as she sucks in a breath.

"Move your hand, Viktor," she demands.

I move my hand higher up her thigh. "Is that better?" I ask teasingly.

"That's... that's not what I meant," she stutters.

"Are you sure it's not? Because the way your body is reacting to my touch makes me think you want me to move my hand up higher and sink my fingers deep inside your pussy like I did in my office."

"Do it, and I'll grab the wheel and kill us both," she threatens.

She might actually do it, too. I remove my hand from her thigh, not because I'm afraid of her killing us like she said, but I plan on teasing her more at dinner.

We arrive at the restaurant, and Violet's out of the car before I get a chance to open the door for her—stubborn woman. We enter Géfsi tis Elládas. Taste of Greece. The hostess shows us to our table, and I pull out Violet's chair for her. She gives me a dirty look, and I give her a charming smile back, scooting her closer to the table.

I take my seat. "Would you like a bottle of wine?" I ask her.

"No, I don't drink," she states.

Hm, interesting. "Do you mind if I do?" I ask, not wanting to offend her if she's not comfortable with me drinking.

"I don't care," she replies, emotionless.

The waitress comes to our table, and I order whatever beer they have on the menu. She brings it to me and I take a sip. It's no Baltika, but it will do. Violet stares at my beer with an uncomfortable look on her face. I look at the mug, trying to figure out what has made her so uncomfortable all of a sudden.

"Is my beer offending you, Violet?" I ask.

She finally looks away from my beer to me. "No, it's fine, sorry."

She relaxes back in her seat, but she's clearly still upset about the beer. I could care less about it, so if it's upsetting her, I will get rid of it. I call our waitress over.

"Is everything okay, sir?" the woman asks.

"No, please take my beer and bring me some water."

"Yes, of course," she says , taking my beer with her.

Violet immediately relaxes. "You didn't need to do that. I told you you can drink, I just don't like beer."

Raising one eyebrow at her, I question her. "Why do you not like beer?"

She looks uncomfortable again. "My father was an alcoholic, and beer was his drink of choice."

"You said it was? Has your father passed?" I ask.

"I'm not talking to you about my parents, Viktor."

I've clearly struck a nerve asking her that, yet I can't help but need to know more about them, about everything from her past. Then it hits me how I can ease her into giving me even a little peek into her life.

"Fine, since this is my favor, I want five questions answered as part of it," I say, hoping she will go along with it.

"Fine, five questions, that's all you get, then you don't ask me any for the rest of the night," she says.

"Agreed."

I rub at my jawline, thinking hard about the first question, not wanting to upset her and ruin the date by talking about her parents which is obviously a sore subject for her.

"When was your last date?" I ask, curious to know why a woman as enticing as her has stayed single.

"Five years ago," she replies.

I'm stunned it's been that long. "Why?"

"You only get five questions, Viktor. Do you really care why?"

"Yes," I say honestly.

"Fine. I haven't dated in five years because I rather get hit by a fucking train than get my heart broken again. Love is a weakness to me now, and I have no interest in being weak again," she states.

"I don't think you would ever be perceived as being weak, Violet."

She looks away from me and down at the table. I want to ask her more about her past relationships, how exactly she got hurt, maybe a list of the names of the men that did it. But I put those questions aside for now. I want to know more about her family first.

"You mentioned your father drank often, but what about your mother?" I ask.

Violet grips her water glass tightly. "I don't have a mother. I have a woman that gave birth to me, and that's all you need to know."

I nod. "Fair enough." *Don't mention Mom again, got it.* On to the next question, then. "What's something no one knows about you?"

"There's a lot people don't know about me, Viktor."

"Just pick one," I sigh.

"I own a house just outside of New York, although I guess someone else besides you knows about it."

Right. I remember her mentioning on the phone last night about some men coming to her house. I want to ask her more about this, but I only have one question left, so it will have to wait. "Last question, Viktor, you better make it a good one," she says.

"Okay, I'll let you have the option of choosing between two questions. Question one: how many times have you touched yourself to the thought of me eating your pussy?" I ask, not even bothering to hide the hunger in my voice. "And question two: how wet are you for me right now?"

Giving me a flirtatious glance, Violet leans in closer to the table. "I'll take question two—as dry as the fucking desert."

She leans back in her chair with a smartass smile on her face, like she's won. She hasn't. Violet hasn't realized that eyes can talk, and even though on the outside hers perceive hatred toward me, the more I look into them, all I see is want for me—for us.

"Really? Hmm." I lean in closer just like she did, my chest hitting the table. "If I stick my hand under this table and up your dress to find your pussy soaking wet for me, I will bend you over this table in front of all these people, and show you what happens when you lie to me," I threaten her.

I'm getting hard just thinking about flipping her dress over and seeing her perfect heart-shaped ass. Of course I would never let a bunch of strangers see parts of her that are mine, but she doesn't need to know that. I want her to get it through her head that no matter what she throws at me, I'll fight back. I'm not some weak man that will run away from her fiery spirit.

"Go ahead," she challenges.

I stand and slowly approach Violet. I grab the back of her neck, and she sucks in a breath. Bending down, I bring my lips to her skin, gently kissing it. Her pulse quickens the longer my lips linger there, and I smirk when I lift my lips away. She's turned on; the little liar thinks she's hiding it from me.

"Excuse me for a moment," I tell her, heading over to speak with our waitress to pay for my beer.

Fuck dinner; the only thing I'm interested in eating right now is Violet. I pay the waitress and give her a generous tip for wasting her time. Violet is sipping on her water as I approach our table.

"Dinner's over," I announce.

"Awe, so soon?" she mocks, pretending to pout. "I was actually building up quite the appetite."

"We can order food later, we're going to my place."

"I'm not going to your place, Viktor, the favor was to take me to dinner."

"Well I'm changing it to dinner at my place instead."

"That's not how this works," she seethes, and her eyes bore into me, cold and wild.

"Really? Shall I call Marco and tell him how you made a scene at my club? I only told him what you did to Igor. I never said anything about intruding on my territory without an invitation, but I can if you would like?"

"Are you seriously blackmailing me right now?" she says, now furious with me. I give her a stern look back, letting her know I meant it.

She huffs out an angry breath. "Fuck sakes," Violet says, standing up, her chair scraping forcefully across the floor.

"Good girl," I call her while grabbing her arm and guiding her out of the restaurant.

Her face reddens, and I think she might have liked that I called her a good girl. I tuck that bit of information away for later. I have only seen a glimpse into a few of Violet's kinks, but I intend to uncover more of them tonight.

In the car on our way to my place, Violet is eerily quiet, and I don't like it. "If you're really not comfortable, I can drop you off at Marco's," I offer.

She turns her head to look at me; her need for me is written all over her face. Violet reaches over the center console and places her hand on my cock. I might be wearing dress pants, but the heat from her hand is blissful. I was half hard when we got in the car but am now rock solid from her touch.

"Violet, don't start something you don't plan on finishing," I warn her.

She smirks and rubs her hand up and down my length, teasing me. I grab her hand, stopping the motion while keeping my eyes on the road. I kiss the palm of her hand, her finger tips, and place her hand back into her lap. From the corner of my eye, Violet's clearly pissed I didn't let her continue.

"It's cute you think you are still in control," I tell her.

She turns her attention to the window. "That's fine, just wait until we get back to your place," she mumbles.

"What was that?" I ask, knowing full well what she said.

"I said, I can't wait to get to your place," she says in a sexy tone, but it's fake; she's trying too hard on purpose.

I don't know what Violet has planned, but whatever it is, I'm not sure

I'll enjoy it. I pull into the driveway. I told my men to make themselves scarce tonight, because I planned on bringing her back here, and I didn't want my men hearing or seeing anything. I'm already short a few from the cartel, so killing them for hearing me make Violet scream would put a damper on things.

Violet is out the door faster than me. "Can you hurry up? I really have to pee," she says. She did drink a lot of water at the restaurant, so I'm not surprised.

I punch in my alarm code and open the door, the motion detection lights coming on as we enter. "There's a washroom across the hall there," I say, pointing in its direction.

"Thanks," she replies, slipping off her heels and padding to the washroom.

I remove my shoes as well and take off my navy suit jacket. I lay it over the couch while taking off my cufflinks and roll up my sleeves. Violet is taking quite a long time to pee. I walk toward the bathroom to check on her. As I approach the door, the shower turns on.

"Violet," I call, knocking on the door.

She doesn't respond. I open the door, steam fills the room, and the shower is visible but not Violet. I turn my head to the right, and Violet is standing against the sink, looking as tempting as ever.

"I thought maybe we could take a shower?" she says softly. "I've never had shower sex, and this looks like the perfect shower to do it in." She sounds so innocent.

She's right; it's not an overly big shower, but it has shower heads on either side. I'm a fool for thinking there isn't a reason she's doing this besides wanting me to fuck her. Violet wouldn't make it that easy, but I'm so hard for her right now; the idea of her naked, wet body clinging to mine while I'm deep inside her has me ready to blow my load right on the bathroom floor.

"So what are you waiting for, malyshka? You want to shower, then let's shower. Take your dress off," I order.

"You first, I want to watch you undress."

That sensual tone of hers goes straight to my cock. I wouldn't be able to deny her anything right now even if I tried. I start unbuttoning my dress shirt, and Violet watches every move. Once the shirt is off, I toss it on the tiled floor and start undoing my belt. My pants are next to go along with my briefs. Violet stares obscenely at my cock while biting her lip. My cock isn't massive; it's seven and a half inches. Any bigger and I would be afraid of ripping poor Violet in half. I want her to feel me for days, not end up with a broken pelvis.

"Your turn, malyshka," I say.

"I didn't say I was done watching you yet," she teases.

"Do you remember what I said in the car about me being the one in control?"

"You can be in control after, I promise, just please let me watch you for a little longer. It makes me wet watching you," she says, breathless.

Fuck... Satana day mne sily. *Satan give me strength.* I enter the shower, the hot water doing nothing to calm my already heated skin. If Violet wants to watch, then what kind of man would I be to deny her that pleasure? I let the water run over my face, grabbing some body wash and lather some into my hand, then rub it all over my chest. I make my way down.

Violet watches me through the glass doors as I stroke my cock, getting it nice and clean for her. I tilt my head back slightly, getting lost in the feel of my hand stroking myself for her. So lost in my pleasure, I don't notice Violet move closer to the shower doors. She stands right in front of them, and I rub my hand across the fogged up glass, making it clear enough for me to look at her. I stare into Violet's lust-filled eyes, getting lost in them.

My attention is disrupted by the sound of clanging metal. Confused, I shift my gaze from her face and look down. The little hellion picked up my belt while I was distracted with my cock and tied the fucking shower doors together! I look back up at Violet. She starts backing away from the shower doors with a mischievous smirk on her face, her doe eyes turning dark.

"Violet, untie my belt from the door!" I order.

"Awe, it's cute you think you're the one still in control," she says, throwing my words back in my face. "You know what, Viktor? You're always saying I need to be punished, but I think it's your turn. After all, you did lie to me about Igor."

"I told you not to ever say his fucking name," I say with clenched teeth, trying to control my anger.

"Tsk tsk, Viktor, I don't like your tone." She taunts me like I'm a misbehaving child.

"You're not gonna like what's going to happen if you don't open this fucking door."

"Maybe I will. I told you, Viktor, there's a lot you don't know about me." Oh, I know exactly what she likes and what game she's playing. "When you ate my pussy in your office, you withheld my orgasm from me, and while I'll admit it was the best orgasm I have ever had, it was torture not being able to come, so I'm going to give you a taste of your own medicine."

I clench my jaw. Violet slowly moves both straps of her dress, letting them fall down her shoulders. She pulls the rest of her dress down her body, and I watch as it slides down her hips, pooling at her feet. Violet is now completely naked. I keep rubbing the glass so it doesn't fog up. Fuck this stupid shower.

I switch the water off. "Violet, I'm giving you one more chance to untie the handles and let me out before I break the glass and free myself!"

She ignores me and slowly walks over to the bathroom counter. Violet hops on top of it, placing her feet up and spreading her legs wide open, showing me her perfect pussy. She leans back with one hand and moves her other hand to her clit. The little vixen has locked me in the shower so she can play with herself and make me watch. Does she really not think I will break this glass to get to her? I would break a hundred glass doors with my own fucking fists to get to her. Clearly, Violet underestimates me and hasn't thought her plan through—or maybe that's exactly what she wants me to do. She wants my anger, my roughness, my domination.

"Violet, I swear to fuck! Open this door, or I'll fuck you so hard you won't be able to walk for weeks!" I warn her.

A dangerous smirk forms on her face. She brings the hand that was playing with her pussy up to her face, turning it over and sticking her middle finger up at me, then brings that finger to her lips and licks it seductively while keeping her eyes trained on me. It then travels down her stomach and back to her clit. She rubs herself and moans softly from her own touch. *Trakhni menya*, fuck me, she looks hot as hell touching herself. I squeeze my cock trying to get some relief but it does nothing to sedate my hunger for this woman. I'm like a starved animal; I need to be inside her. Violet rubs her pussy harder, getting lost in her pleasure.

"Violet, don't you dare come!" I demand.

The first time she comes tonight will be on my cock, not on her own hand. She leans back further and rests her head on the mirror, and taking her other hand, she sticks her middle finger up at me again. I clench my jaw, banging on the glass and trying to pull the doors open. The belt stretches around the handles but still doesn't budge. Violet is close to coming, her eyes now closed and her moans getting louder. I ram my shoulder into the glass doors over and over again, shouting Violet's name. Her mouth opens, and a loud moan spills from her lips.

Just as she reaches her orgasm, I kick the door open with such force that both handles break off and fly across the room. Violet's eyes fly open in shock, and she quickly hops off the counter as I storm over to her. She tries to make a run for the door, but I grab her arm and throw her into the edge of the counter, her hip hitting it forcefully. I grab a fistful of her hair and pull her head back toward me.

"Where do you think you're going, malyshka?" I ask, lining my cock up at her entrance. "I told you I don't play games."

I enter her pussy in one harsh thrust. Violet cries out. I give her a few seconds to adjust to my cock then begin fucking her roughly. Her pussy feels better than I imagined it would. I've thought about fucking Violet from the first moment she entered my club and finally being inside her is like fucking heaven.

I arch her back more by pulling harder on her hair, her plump ass bouncing and hitting my lower stomach each time I thrust into her. Violet's moans fill the room, and the louder she moans, the harder I fuck her. I want her screaming and begging for me to make her come. I glance down, and watch my cock slide in and out of her tight pussy; her wet, pink walls sucking my length back deep inside her each time I pull out. I look back up at Violet, her eyes beginning to close from pleasure.

I spank her ass and grab her jaw, forcing her head to face the mirror. "Don't close your eyes, Violet, I want you to watch me own this fucking pussy, because it's mine now, understand?" I growl. Violet watches me fuck her in the mirror and nods. I spank her ass again, harder. "Not good enough, I wanna hear you say it! Who owns this pussy, Violet?" I ask.

"You," she moans, barely getting the full word out.

"Good girl," I call her, biting down hard on her shoulder.

She winces from the bite but then moans. Her arousal drips from her pussy, soaking my balls in her wetness. Fuck, I need to taste her. I pull my cock out and spin her around, lifting her ass up onto the counter. Spreading her legs open, I bend down, giving her pussy one slow lick, curling and flicking my tongue up when I get to her clit. Her sweet wetness coats my tongue, making me more ravenous for her. I stand and drive into her pussy again.

"Fuck!" she screams. I rub her clit while fucking her. Violet looks down between us, watching my cock pump in and out of her pussy; my little freak does love to watch. I rub her clit faster. "Oh, fuck, Viktor! I'm gonna come!" she moans. I take my hand off her pussy and slow my thrusts. "What are you doing?" she asks, breathless.

"Beg me to let you come, malyshka."

She slaps my shoulder hard. "Ugh, I hate you!" she grunts.

"Really?" I thrust my cock as deep as I can inside her, not leaving a single inch out. She gasps. "It doesn't seem like you hate me, Violet."

She slaps me in the face, my head snapping back from the force. I grab her by the throat with one hand, pull out my cock and slap her pussy hard with the other, then enter her again.

She cries out from the slap. "Ah, fuck!"

"I can do this all night, Violet," I tell her.

I begin thrusting slowly in and out of her pussy again, teasing her. I bend down to her breasts, taking one in my mouth, sucking and biting it, torturing her more.

She moans in frustration. "Fuck, fine, you win. Please, can I come, Viktor?!"

Mhm, when she begs, it's the sweetest sound I've ever heard on this god forsaken earth. If I could hear one sound for the rest of my life, it would be that.

I thrust faster inside her, placing my hand back on her clit and rubbing it. "Come for me, Violet," I tell her.

She closes her eyes, and I apply more pressure to my hand around her throat. Her pussy clenches around my cock as she comes and I kiss her, swallowing her scream of pleasure. Being inside Violet for the first time was like heaven, but kissing her is euphoric. I deepen the kiss while fucking her hard through her orgasm. My balls draw up tight, my own release getting ready. I break our kiss and wrap Violet's legs around my waist, bringing her closer to me. Gripping both her legs, fucking her so hard that she's definitely going to be sore tomorrow. Violet places a hand between us and starts rubbing her pussy while I fuck her.

Fuck, seeing Violet get herself off while my cock is inside her undoes me. I grunt loudly, releasing my load. My vision blurs, and I drop Violet's legs, both of us panting and out of breath. I rest my forehead on hers, trying to control my breathing. Once we both catch our breath, I slide my cock out of her pussy. Violet winces, and I would say I feel bad, but I don't. I watch as my cum pours out of her pussy, trickling down to her ass and onto the counter. Watching my load leak out of her has me getting hard and ready to fuck her again, but I was rough with her and should let her rest... for now.

I grab a washcloth from the drawer beside me and move to the side, closer to the sink. I run the washcloth under warm water, ringing it out after. Moving toward Violet, she tries grabbing it from me.

"You tried that once before and you remember my answer," I tell her. She smiles, rolling her eyes at me. I place her feet on the counter and stand between her open legs. "Look at this swollen little pussy from me fucking it so hard," I say, placing a kiss on it.

The warmth from the cloth soothes her. Violet sighs as I gently wipe it over her sensitive skin, cleaning her. I toss the cloth in the sink and grab Violet's legs, lifting her off the counter and carrying her bridal style out of the bathroom.

"Where are we going?" she questions.

"Upstairs to shower, since someone made me break the one down here," I reply.

She giggles. "Don't blame me for that, you could've just been patient, I was going to let you out eventually," she says with a sassy little smirk.

"I'm not a patient man, Violet."

She snorts. "Yeah, I'm starting to get that."

I shake my head at her. Violet seems surprisingly calm and playful after what we just did. I expected her to be closed off and distant as soon as we were done, like she normally is, but I know this is only temporary. By tomorrow, she'll be back to being cold and denying her feelings for me, so I'm going to enjoy this side of her while I still can.

We make it upstairs to my ensuite bathroom. I set Violet down on her feet and turn on the shower. This shower has double showerheads, too, but is bigger and only has one sliding door, so Violet can't get any more ideas about locking me in and running away. I grab Violet's hand and walk with her into the shower, sliding the door closed behind us. I put some body wash on a washcloth and start rubbing it across her shoulders. I study the few scars she has on her body, much like mine. She's clearly good at what she does, or she would have a lot more scars. The thought of her killing other men turns me on; it shouldn't, but then again, everything she does seems to.

"You know, I'm more than capable of washing myself," she says.

"Just let me take care of you, just for tonight. Don't fight me on it."

She must see the need to care for her in my eyes, because she doesn't fight me. I continue to wash her, moving the cloth across her chest and down her stomach, when a thought crosses my mind; *we didn't use protection. Shit.* I know Violet hasn't been with any men in five years, but I want to free her mind of worry about me.

"I haven't had sex with anyone in a few months, and I get tested frequently, so I'm clean, and if you're worried about getting pregnant, I had a vasectomy last year," I reassure her.

She smiles. "I wasn't worried about getting pregnant. I'm on the pill, but thank you for telling me," she says.

I squint at her, confused. "Why are you on birth control if you haven't been with a man in years?"

She rolls her eyes. "There are other reasons women take birth control, Viktor. It helps regulate periods, and if—god forbid—something were to happen and I got raped, I wouldn't be forced to have my rapist's evil spawn in me. Something men never have to worry about," she says angrily.

"You can stop taking it, you don't need it with me, and I know it can ruin a woman's body; I would never let anyone touch you, Violet," I tell her.

I would die protecting Violet, and even then I would find a way to crawl out from hell to save her, even if I had to use the devil's corpse to dig my way out.

"I don't need your protection, Viktor, I can protect myself. I have been doing it for years," she replies, a slight hint of pain in her voice.

"So let me do it now," I press, looking down at her.

She looks up at me, our eyes meeting. "I can't," she whispers.

There's such sadness in her hazel eyes, I trace the pad of my thumb along her wet cheek. "Teper' ty moy, moy slomannyy angel. Prinimayesh' ty eto ili net." *You are mine now, my broken angel, whether you accept it or not.*

"You know, one day, I'm going to learn Russian so you can't hide your words from me."

"I'm not hiding them, you just aren't ready to hear them yet."

I pull her into my chest and kiss the top of her head as water cascades down on us. Tomorrow, she may hate me again, hate how her feelings have changed for me, but there's one thing that won't: Violet's mine, and nothing she says or does can change that.

CHAPTER 14
Weaknesses

Violet

I LEFT VIKTOR'S after we showered and almost fucked again. He gave me a change of clothes; another shirt of his I can add to the first one he gave me. He wanted me to stay, and a part of me did, too, but I couldn't. To my surprise, I'm getting attached to him, and sleeping in his bed would just make things worse. I can't believe I let myself get involved with a man. I swore to myself I would never go through the same hurt I did with my past relationships. For years, I stuck to it, until Viktor came along and fucked it all up.

I never thought I inherited my parents addictive genes, but when it comes to him, I clearly did. He's like a drug I can't go a day without wanting or thinking about. It makes it even harder to shake those urges when he looks at me the way he did while taking care of me in the shower, like I actually mean something to him. Viktor isn't supposed to see me as some fragile doll. I worked too hard to be the woman I am today to still seem broken. I shared too much of my mind and body with him. I'm not sure what came over me, but it's hard saying no to that man. It's so easy to come undone around him, and I can't fucking stand it. He messed with my head and made me feel comfortable enough to share pieces of me I haven't shared with anyone in years.

I get out of bed, wincing when my legs open. Jesus, that man destroyed my pussy last night. It's the best sex I've ever had; he's so good at playing with my body exactly how he wants, how I need him to. Locking him in the shower with his belt was on a total whim, but when he denied me touching him in the car, I lost it. I wanted to punish him for making me willingly give up my control. I have never been a submissive woman, but when Viktor speaks, my brain turns to mush, and I do things I wouldn't normally do.

I walk to the washroom and splash some cold water on my face, trying to clear my head and wake myself up. My body hurts more from getting fucked by Viktor than it does when I fight a man. Despite my sore muscles protesting against it, I do my yoga. I'm flying out to Italy today to visit my family, and I'm hoping I'll be too busy with them to think about Viktor for a few days. A text comes through while doing pyramid pose, and I flip my phone over to see it's from Maison.

> Hey boss, you're not mad at me, are you? Just haven't heard from you.

Part of me wants to reply that I've been too busy getting my pussy and feelings fucked. But I never share personal life matters with Maison.

> Sorry, I've just been busy, I was going to message you before I fly to Italy. Marco and Viktor have both been hit hard by this cartel gang, they can't seem to figure out this group's whereabouts. They wear black masks, but they all have the same tattoo on their wrists.

I send Maison an image of the tattoo.

> While I'm away, see what you can find out about them and where they might be hiding.

> Sure, can do, boss lady! I'll see what I can dig up. Enjoy your trip!

Thanks.

Hopefully Maison can find something. Marco has been spending long nights trying to find these men, and I'm sure Viktor's been doing the same.

I dress and get ready for my flight, glancing at my phone while I zip up my suitcase. I can't help but feel a little disappointed that Viktor hasn't reached out to me yet.

Oh who cares, Violet, the man fucked you. He doesn't need to text you to see how you're doing, and you shouldn't want him to.

It was just sex, that's all. *Control your emotions,* I say to myself while taking a deep breath in and out, forgetting about him already. I've never lied to myself this much in one day.

MY PLANE LANDS in Milan Bergamo airport. It's the closest airport to Lombardy, a forty-five minute drive to Marco's. His driver picks me up and while in the car looking at the beautiful Italian scenery, my phone dings. To my horror, my heart skips a beat—it's Viktor.

How are you feeling this morning, moy slomannyy angel, sore?

I can't help but smile at his text. Another Russian nickname I noticed he likes to call me. I'm not sure what 'moy slomannyy angel' means. I could look it up, but I want Viktor to tell me the meaning behind it, and why he calls me that.

> Yes, very. As if you aren't the least bit proud of that.

What am I doing? Am I actually flirting with Viktor right now?

> Good, I want your pussy to always remember how good my cock felt inside her.

Fuck, getting wet on the way to see my family definitely wasn't on my agenda.

> She does, I don't think I could make her forget even if I tried.

And that's one hundred percent true. I've been trying to forget about last night all morning, and now here I am, sexting Viktor about it.

> Where are you right now?

> Why?

> Just answer the question, Violet.

Viktor's demanding side turns me on, but it also rubs me the wrong way. If he thinks because we fucked he can boss me around like I'm his bitch, he's dead wrong.

> It's none of your business where I am! We fucked, Viktor, that's it. It doesn't mean you're entitled to know where I am.

You know, I thought I fucked the attitude out of you, but apparently not. I'll have to fuck you harder next time.

You can try.

Tell me where you are and I will.

Good luck with that, unless you are planning on hopping on a plane to come and find me, you won't have much luck.

Let me guess, Italy?

Nope, I'm in Russia, turning your own people against you. I think I'll start my own Bratva so I can overrun yours.

You can try ;) Seriously, Violet, tell me where you are, I'm getting impatient.

You're a smart man, Viktor, figure it out.

He doesn't respond, and honestly, I'm glad. We just arrived at the mansion, and I can't walk in there all red-faced and flustered from one of Viktor's dirty texts.

The mansion is oddly quiet. It's never quiet in here, not since Lily was born. Even before then, the girls are always laughing and playing music.

I drop my bags at the door. "Hello?" I yell, my voice echoing throughout the mansion.

Nothing. Not a single soul answers. Did they forget I was coming? Getting a little worried, I continue deeper into the mansion. Nothing seems out of place, and the guards are all posed at their normal stations. I walk toward the gym, and loud music is playing from inside the room. When I head inside, Dante's sparring with a punching bag hanging from the ceiling, completely focused. Sneaking up behind him when he goes for a left hook, I grab his arm and flip him over onto his back.

"What the fuck?!" he yells, disorientated.

I loom over him laying on the ground. "What happened to never letting your guard down, asshat?" I tease.

When we trained, Dante would tell me to never let my guard down, not even for a second, yet he's over here blasting music, home alone, where anyone could have killed the guards, walked in here and took him out.

"Shit, my bad, V. I forgot you were coming today," he says sheepishly, getting up from the gym floor.

"Wow, thanks," I reply with a mocking tone.

Dante pauses his music, the room now quiet. "Come on, now, I didn't mean it like that. It just slipped my mind. Things have been tense around here lately. Marco and I have been up late every night the past few weeks looking for that cartel gang, and Nikki has been busy with Lily's dance recital. Sabrina's been busy making her costume—" he rambles.

"I get it, I was joking, Dante. You know me better than that, I just wasn't expecting to arrive at an empty house."

"Yeah, sorry about that. Nikki's at Lily's dance practice, and Sabrina and Marco are out getting groceries for family dinner tonight; they should be back soon," he explains.

Lily has inherited her mother's love for dance, though their dance styles are completely different. Nikki never took ballet, but Lily loves it, and she looks adorable in her little tutu. Her first recital's next week, and Nikki has been stressing herself out making sure everything is perfect for it.

"Since it's just us for a bit, do you wanna train together? It will be like old times—me hitting a bag, you throwing your little knives at a board," he says, poking fun at me.

"Those little knives can do a hell of a lot more damage than you think, especially if I put one through the top of your skull," I say, smiling at him.

"Not sure my wife would like that."

"Eh, I could find her a new husband in a week, she would be fine," I reply, teasing him.

"Nah, I hired a hitman to kill any man that tries to get with my wife if I'm dead." He grins.

I wouldn't be surprised if Dante is telling the truth. Both he and Marco are the most obsessive men I've ever met when it comes to their wives; they wouldn't let another man near them, not even after their deaths.

"So, what do you say?" he asks.

"Honestly, I can use some training, might help clear my head."

I take my jacket off. It was cold on the plane, but it's hot in Italy, so I wore a black tank top underneath.

Facing Dante, he stares at my shoulder. "Holy shit, Red, you have a bite mark!"

My hand touches where he's looking. *Fucking Viktor!* My cheeks flush with embarrassment. How did I not notice? *Think, Violet, make something up!* Dante and Marco can't find out about Viktor and me.

"Oh, yeah, I killed this guy last night, real mean bastard. He must have bitten me while I was stabbing him to death."

I try to keep my expression neutral. Seriously, that's the best I can come up with? I'm amazing at lying; why does this one suck?!

"Fuck, I'm surprised you let him get that close, maybe you do need more training," he says, smirking and throwing his sweaty towel at me .

"Ew, gross! And I'll have you know, my killing skills are the same as they have always been."

"Whatever you say, Red."

I roll my eyes at him and bend down slightly to choose my first knife to throw from the selection of knives on the table. Dante's eyes are on me, and I look up from the table to glance at him standing in front of me.

"What?" I ask.

"So this guy you say you killed... Did he happen to suck on your tits and leave a hickey before you killed him, too?"

I look at him in shock. "What!?"

Checking my chest, sure enough, there's a big purple bruise on the top of my right breast that thankfully is only visible when I bend down.

"Fucking fuck!" I hiss, frustrated.

"That's what I wanna know. Don't tell me you finally got lucky after five years, Violet, and didn't tell me!"

"Please don't make this a bigger deal than it is, I'm already not happy about it."

"Awe shit, was it bad? Did he have a small dick?" he teases.

I laugh. *Nope, definitely not small.* "No, it was good. Too good, and I rather just pretend it didn't happen, so can we move on and train, please?" I ask.

"Fuck no, Violet, this is huge! Since I've known you, the only time you ever let a man anywhere near you is when you plan on killing him. This is the first time you've had dick in five years! I wanna know who it was, unless you have killed him already," he jokes.

"Oh my god, you sound like a girl wanting details about my sex life."

"Wow, slow down there, I never said details—you're my sister. We may not share blood, but still… Keep your fetishes to yourself. I'm just curious who the guy was that finally made you crack," he says. "Wait, Marco said you owed a favor to Viktor. He didn't do this to you as his favor, did he? Because I swear to god, if you didn't kill him, I will!" He's suddenly pissed off, so I quickly ease his suspicions.

"No, no, you think I would go through with something like that? It just happened, and it was one time, that's it. It will never happen again."

Dante squints at me. "You don't sound very convinced about that."

"Well, I am! It can't happen again, even if I want it to."

"Hold on, V, do you like him?" he asks, tone softening.

I snort. "What am I, in high school? No! I don't like him."

"Okay, my bad! Do you have feelings for him? Is that a more age-appropriate question?" he asks, rolling his eyes.

"No, Dante! You know I don't do that shit. We have talked about this many times; I have no interest in being with a man, in love or any of the bullshit that comes with it."

"V, it's been years. I understand your reasoning behind it. I used to be the same, remember? But you were the one that changed my mind on the idea of love."

"That's different, Dante, you thought being in love and getting married was a waste of time. That shackling yourself to one woman sounded like hell. You didn't believe in love, but I do. Just not for me," I say regretfully.

"Do you hear how dumb you sound?"

"Watch it! Just because you're my brother doesn't mean I won't stab you!"

"I mean it, Violet, you really think Marco and I were deserving of love with all the shit we have done? The people we have killed?"

"You're still good men," I say softly, not meeting his gaze.

"And you're a good woman, Red. Viktor would be lucky to call you his."

I sigh. "Dante, enough. I'm not having this conversation with you any longer."

"Fine. It's your choice, be a bitter old woman all alone, Violet, but I'm going to tell you the same thing you told me when I was having doubts about my feelings for Nikki: don't come crying to me when you realize the mistake you're making, and you end up losing Viktor."

Dante storms out of the gym. I grab a knife off the table and throw it angrily at the target, hitting dead center. Dante doesn't understand. What he and Nikki have, I could never have with Viktor, even if I wanted to. It would never work out between us. Viktor would eventually leave me and find the woman he's meant to be with. They always do. I was always a temporary placeholder in a man's life, and Viktor won't be the next man to do it to me again.

Later that night, after finishing dinner with the family, I'm tired as fuck. I crawl into bed and relax into the mattress. Dante didn't say a word to me at dinner. I don't understand why he cares so much about Viktor and me. Laying on my side, I close my eyes and start to drift off, but I'm woken by a sudden pressure on my bed. I grab the knife I keep hidden under my pillow and swing my arm in front of me, but someone grabs it mid-swing. My eyes try to adjust to the darkness so I can see who.

"Hello, moy slomannyy angel."

CHAPTER 15
No Games

Viktor

IT'S DARK IN Violet's room, but the window casts a moonlight glow, allowing me to see Violet's face. Her wide eyes stare back at me, shocked. I'm getting hard already, having her beneath me like this.

"Viktor, what the fuck are you doing here?" she shouts.

"I told you I was getting impatient," I growl, smirking down at her.

"How the hell did you find me? And get off!"

She squirms, her hips bucking upward and bumping into my cock, trying to get me off her.

"It wasn't hard, I called Marco to see if you were here."

"Wow, great detective work," she says sarcastically.

Her hips rub against my length again. "If you don't stop moving on my cock, I'll be forced to bury it inside your warm pussy," I grunt out.

"Not happening. If you get off me, I will stop. Either that, or let go of my hand so I can stab you off me."

I grab the knife and throw it across the room, then grip her jaw. "What did I tell you about this attitude of yours?" I growl. She's silent, but has a telling look on her face. She knows exactly what I'm talking about. "If I remember correctly, I said I need to do a better job at fucking it out of you."

I run the pad of my thumb across her lower lip. Violet goes to bite the tip, but I pull away before she has the chance.

Gripping her jaw tighter, I bring her head up from her pillow and closer to me. "Bad girl, I think I'll start now," I snap, grabbing a fistful of her hair and pulling it to guide her off the bed and onto the bedroom floor, onto her knees. The moonlight makes her look like a goddess. I wrap her hair around my fist, getting as much out of her face as I can. "Undo my belt, Violet," I demand. She studies me, but makes no move to obey. I tug on her hair, not hard, but enough to get her attention. "Now, Violet," I order, my voice husky. She reluctantly unbuckles my belt, her fingers slowly undoing my button and zipper afterward. "Now take my cock out."

Her warm hands reach into my briefs and pull my cock free. It bobs in front of her face, and Violet subtly licks her lips as I smile. "Do you want my cock in your mouth, Violet?" I rasp. She shakes her head, giving me a defiant look. I bring her face closer to the head of my cock. "Still with the attitude," I say, reaching my hand down to her breast and pinching her nipple through her thin tank top. She moans then winces when I pinch it harder. "Be a good girl and open your mouth for me." I keep my voice light.

"I think we both know I'm not a good girl, Viktor," she says seductively.

"For me, you are. Now open your mouth, so I can feed you my cock."

Violet opens her mouth for me, and I slowly inch my length inside. Her lips stretch around my girth, and she looks up at me from beneath her lashes. Her beautiful eyes fill with lust as she takes me deeper into her mouth. *Fuck.* The head of my cock hits the back of her throat, and I nearly come just from the warmth and the way she's looking at me.

Violet takes control, suctioning her mouth around my cock and bobbing her head up and down, never breaking eye contact. "Mhm, that's it, malyshka. Take my cock deeper down your throat," I groan.

She does more than that. Violet's pupils dilate. She takes both her hands and slowly moves them up and down in rhythm with her sucking. *Jesus Christ.* She's sucking my cock like she needs me to come, like she wants it for her own satisfaction.

"That's it, Violet, good little cocksucker," I growl.

Violet sucks faster and deeper, gagging each time she takes it, choking on my thick cock. Suddenly, she stops. Her lips smirk around my girth. She's trying to stop me from coming.

"Wrong time to try and give me a taste of my own medicine, malyshka."

I smirk back down at her, tightening my fist around her red locks. I take control, and start fucking her mouth. Her eyes begin to water as saliva pours out of her mouth around my cock.

My balls start to draw up, tightening. "Do you want my load down your throat, Violet?" I ask, my voice husky from the pleasure.

Fuck, I'm gonna come so hard. She nods, her mouth full of my cock, and moans deeply. The vibration goes straight to my balls, and I come hard, right down her throat.

"Fuck!" I grunt. My vision goes hazy as the last of my release trickles out from her lips.

Violet is still on her knees, looking up at me. She sticks out her tongue to show me she swallowed every last drop. I didn't even ask her to, which makes the act that much more sexy. Fuck this woman. Pakhans don't get on their knees for anyone. Not our men, our family, especially not our enemies... But fuck, I would get on my knees for her, just as she is for me now, in front of all my men if she begged me to, not giving a single fuck how weak it made me look to them.

"Did you enjoy tasting my cum for the first time, Violet?" I ask. She nods, her lips red and face flushed. Fuck, she looks beautiful. "Good girl," I praise her. "Now go back to bed."

Her forehead creases. "What?" she shouts. "After what I just did, you expect me to sleep?" She stands and crosses her arms.

I tuck my cock back into my pants and zip them up. "Oh, I'm sorry, were you looking for something in return?" I ask with a smirk.

"Um, damn right I am! You come all the way here from New York, wake me up in the middle of the night, I give you a pornstar blow job, and you think I don't expect to have an orgasm, too?"

I tower over her and back her closer to her bed. "Well, maybe you should have thought about that before you decided to play the guessing game with me, instead of just telling me where you were. Tonight, you can go to bed wet and needy for my touch, and tomorrow, I'll consider giving you an orgasm."

"And people say *I'm* a sadist," she mutters, turning to her bed and crawling into it. Once she's under the covers, I pad over to the armchair with a footrest by the window, facing her bed. "You know I can just get myself off, right? I've been doing it alone for years, it wouldn't take me long," she teases.

"That's why I plan on sleeping right here," I say, sitting in the chair and resting my head on the back of it.

"Seriously, there's like twenty other guest rooms in this place."

"Don't care, I'm perfectly comfortable here. Goodnight, moy slomannyy angel."

Violet rustles in her sheets. "Annoying ass-fucking Russian," she mumbles to herself.

"What was that?" I ask.

"I said goodnight!"

I smile and close my eyes, listening to the sounds of Violet's soft breathing.

I'M WOKEN BY something soft thrown hard at my face. I blink a few times then look down at a navy-blue pillow laying in my lap. This woman just whipped a pillow at my face.

"Morning, sunshine," she says with a sneer.

"Good morning, moy slomannyy angel, did you sleep well?" I ask her, getting up from the chair and stretching my limbs.

That armchair wasn't the worst place I have slept, but it definitely wasn't comfortable. I thought about crawling into bed next to Violet once she was asleep, but I wanted to live to see the morning, so I stayed in the chair.

"I slept fine," she answers, sounding short.

"You seem a little annoyed this morning, Violet. Is it because I didn't make you come last night, or do you miss my cock in your mouth already?" I say, moving away from the chair and closer to her. She's still wearing that thin tank top, and a pair of sleep shorts. Her nipples are getting hard through the fabric of the shirt as I approach her.

"Neither, and now that we have both slept, and it's no longer 2:30 in the fucking morning, why did you fly all the way here, Viktor? And don't tell me it's because you were impatient and needed your dick sucked!" she says in a clipped tone.

I raise an eyebrow. "Did you not enjoy sucking my cock, malyshka?" I say with a grin. She sure as hell didn't seem like she didn't.

"I'm asking the questions now, Viktor. What the hell were you thinking?" she yells.

"I wasn't, I needed to see you. It didn't matter where you were, all I cared about was finding you," I admit.

"Why?! You got plenty of me the night we went to dinner; what more could you possibly want?"

My jaw clenches from holding back my anger. "You think that's the only reason I'm here?" Of course she does. Violet's hatred of men probably stems from a list of shitty exes who just used her for sex. I will not have her think I'm just like them.

"Isn't it?" she asks in an accusatory tone. "Viktor, I told you I don't do this. We had a night of fun, I owed you a favor, and it's done now. There's no need for you to be here."

She's trying to make sense of it all, but she's missing the reason I came; how have I not made my feelings for her clear?

"Are you the forgiving type, Violet?" I ask.

She looks at me, perplexed. "Why are you asking me that?"

"Because I need forgiving."

"For what, exactly?"

"For making you think I don't want you."

Violet's chest rises as she takes in a steady breath. "I know you want me, Viktor," she says.

"No, you don't."

We stare at each other, Violet looking lost in her own thoughts. "I need to get dressed," she says quietly, turning away from me and walking toward her dresser. "Lily, Dante's daughter, will want me to play with her in the garden after breakfast. You can talk with Marco and Dante while I'm with her," she suggests while opening drawers and grabbing clothes from each one.

"I'm not here to intrude on your time with your family, that is not my intention. I wanted to see you, and I have. I planned on leaving this morning," I explain to her.

"Well you came all the way here, at least stay for breakfast."

Warmth blooms in my chest. "If you want me to, I will."

She gives me a small smile that doesn't quite reach her eyes, but it's a smile nonetheless, so I'm counting it as a win. Maybe I am making progress with her. Me coming here was an impulse decision, a need so strong to see Violet that it consumed me, and no obstacle or country was going to keep me from her.

Violet gets ready in the ensuite bathroom while I change into fresh clothes. I only packed a small bag, because I planned on hopping on a plane at dawn. Once I'm dressed in grey dress pants and a black shirt, I take a seat on the edge of Violet's bed to wait for her. It would likely be more awkward if

I walked down there alone. I spoke to Marco before flying here to make sure this was where she was. When he said yes, I asked him if it would be alright if I came to see her, that it was an important matter, and he didn't ask any questions, just told me where the house was and that he would let his men know I'd be arriving late that night.

I found it odd that he didn't ask me what was so urgent that I needed to fly all the way to Italy to see Violet. While I'm thinking of reasons, the bathroom door opens, and Violet enters the room. I'm frozen in place. Her hair is up in a high ponytail, with a black ribbon covered in white polka dots. She's wearing a black crop top, showing me slivers of her bare midriff, and white linen pants with a pair of black flats. Violet looks so relaxed; I haven't seen her dressed this casual before. Violet dressed up in her black leather and tight dresses gets my blood pumping and my cock hard, but casual Violet steals my breath away and takes it for her own.

She catches me staring at her. "What?" she asks.

"Nothing," I reply, unable to stop my smile.

"Why are you staring at me?"

"Because I can."

"I've killed men for looking at me like that. What makes you think you're any different?"

"When I look at you, your body tenses with desire. You pretend to hate it, but you actually love it, whereas when other men do it, it repulses you. Angers you to think they would have the audacity to stare. So, I will stare at you all fucking day, because I can." Violet looks at me, a little stunned. "Now, let's go eat before I decide to keep you up here and eat you for breakfast instead." She rolls her eyes at me, and I lightly spank her ass when she walks in front of me.

She turns sharply around and glares up at me. "Rule number one while you are here: don't touch me in front of anyone!" she whispers angrily as we walk out the bedroom door, heading for the stairs.

I ignore her and watch her ass jiggle as she walks down the steps in front of me. I'm regretting not fucking her last night and giving her that orgasm. I've been dying to watch her ass bounce as I plow into her from behind since we fucked last. I guess I'll have to control my urges until she gets back home to New York.

We make it downstairs to the very extravagant kitchen, with Marco sitting at the table with his laptop and his wife sitting on his lap. Their attention moves away from the screen to us as we enter the kitchen.

"Morning, Violet, Viktor," Marco greets us.

I clear my throat. "Morning," I say, feeling slightly out of place. I have never talked to or seen Marco in a non-business matter, so standing here in his kitchen is a little off-putting.

"Morning, guys," Violet says with her head down, heading to the espresso machine.

She's clearly feeling awkward as well, and guilt gnaws at me for putting her in this position. I needed to see Violet for my own selfish reasons. I don't want her to think she needs to explain things to her family if she doesn't want to.

"So, Viktor, is it?" Marco's wife asks. I nod in her direction. "I'm Sabrina, it's nice to meet you," she says, smiling.

"You too. I'm sorry for intruding. Violet asked me to stay for breakfast, but after that, I'll be on my way back to New York," I reassure her.

"You're not intruding; any friend of Violet's is welcome to stay," she replies, smirking at Violet. Violet's cheeks are flushed as she takes a sip of her coffee.

"Thank you," I say, standing awkwardly near the kitchen island.

"I'm surprised you needed to fly all the way here to see her, must have been important business," Sabrina says, arching a brow.

Marco grabs her hip. I'm guessing it's to signal her to stop asking questions. Before I get to answer, a little voice chimes in, yelling Violet's name. Violet drops her coffee cup, and a little girl who looks about three comes barreling into the kitchen and straight into Violet's arms.

"Aunty Violet!"

"Hi, Lily Pad! Are you ready to make some flower crafts?" Violet asks, smiling down at her.

"Yay!" Lily yells back, jumping up and down in excitement. She turns her head in my direction. "Who's that guy?" she asks, pointing at me. I can't help but laugh at the way she said "that guy."

"Oh, that's Viktor, he's a friend of mine," Violet tells her.

That's the second time the word "friend" is used to describe who I am to Violet, and I can't say I like it.

"Is he gonna make flower crafts with us, too?" Lily asks, looking up at Violet with admiration.

"Ah, no, he's gonna stay here with uncle Marco. I don't think flower crafts are really his thing," she says, giving me a small smile.

"She's right, I'm not the best at crafts, but I bet you are, so how about you make me one with your aunty Violet for me?" I say to her, bending my body down to get closer to her level.

"Okay! We'll make you the best flower craft ever!" she squeals happily, grabbing Violet's hand and pulling her to the door to the back yard. "Let's go, Aunty Violet!"

"Okay, okay, I'm comin'!" Violet says, trying to catch up to her. I'm now alone in the kitchen with Marco and Sabrina.

"I think I'll join them, give you men a chance to talk alone," Sabrina announces, getting up off Marco's lap and heading outside.

Marco stands. "Coffee?" he offers.

"Sure," I reply, walking with him to the machine.

"I can't say I wasn't surprised by your call. I'm not a fool, Viktor, I know nothing could have been that important. Whatever is going on between you and Violet is your business, but I need you to understand one thing: if you hurt her in any way, our peace treaty gets thrown out the fucking window," Marco spits out.

"I understand. I will happily throw myself out there along with it if I ever do," I say. I mean it; I would never intentionally do anything to hurt Violet.

"Good."

He turns to look out the sliding glass doors and leans against the side of the island, sipping his espresso. I do the same, moving closer to the doors to get a better view of Violet outside. The rich espresso goes down smoothly, waking my senses.

"Some days, I wonder how a man like me got so lucky," he admits, eyes focused on Sabrina. Violet and Lily giggle as they twist and tie two flower stems together. "There's a part of me that believes I don't deserve her, but I'm a selfish bastard, because I can't imagine a world without her."

I laugh under my breath. "I understand the feeling."

I know exactly what Marco means. I'm not a horrible man, but I'm not exactly a good one, either. Sometimes, I feel like I'm in way over my head with Violet, but I can't let her go, either.

Violet lets out a big laugh as her and Sabrina both freak out over a bug flying around their faces. God, that laugh. It brings such warmth to my chest. I thought her moaning my name was the greatest sound, but her laugh beats it. That's the first time I've heard her laugh. Everything this woman does surprises me. I thought I had Violet all figured out, but then she does something that makes me feel like I'm not even close to knowing the real her.

But I think I see her now; this is the real Violet. Under the hurt, the pain, the killing, the sassy attitude. There's a happy woman. Loving and carefree. She can be herself here, not like in New York. In New York, she has her heart on guard, and she is working, saving women. Here in Italy, she can be free. I continue watching her with Lily, ingraining this happy image of her in my mind. I might not get to see her like this again, so I'm soaking it all up now. Lost in the sight of her, I don't hear Dante enter the room and come up beside me.

"Viktor, I didn't expect you here, is there something going on?" he asks with slight worry in his tone.

"No, I—"

Marco interrupts us. "Perfect, you're here, Dante. It's your turn to have the protective brother talk with Viktor. I have work to do," he says, leaving the two of us.

Great. This should be fun. I get the feeling Dante is more protective over Violet just from the way he's staring me down.

"I'm sure Marco has already had the 'Don't hurt Violet, or I will kill you' speech, but I'm not worried about you hurting her," he says.

"Thank you."

"Because I know before we got to you, you would already be dead."

I give a small laugh. "You're not wrong."

"But I will say this: Violet won't be an easy woman to love, but she will be worth it. It's pretty obvious you know that already."

I look at him, a bit surprised. "Who said I love her?" I ask.

"No one. I can just tell you are. You look at her the same way I look at Nikki, like you would burn down the world just to make her smile."

He's right; I am falling in love with Violet. I have never been in love before, in all my years as Pakhan, I was too focused on my duties to ever really think about finding love. A wife, a companion, yes, but not love. Of course the one woman I end up falling for has to be one that hates men and hides her emotions like they're a deep dark secret no one can know about.

"How long are you staying?" Dante asks.

"I was thinking of leaving soon, actually. I'm sure Violet is growing more uncomfortable with me still being here."

"Hmm," is all he responds with, and he looks deep in thought as Violet and Lily come running inside.

"Here you go, Viktor!" Lily says excitedly, standing on her tippy toes and reaching out with some sort of flower contraption.

"Wow, that's beautiful, thank you," I tell her, taking the item from her hands.

"Hi, Daddy," she says with a smile, hugging Dante's legs.

"Hi, sweet girl." Dante hugs her back. "Where's Mommy?"

"I'm right here," Nikki says, entering the kitchen.

Lily is the spitting image of her mother. She has Dante's hair colour, but her facial features resemble Nikki's.

"Mommy! Mommy! You missed craft time!" Lily yells, pouting.

"Aw, I know, I'm sorry, sweetie," Nikki says, pinching her cheek.

"That's okay, come on, Mommy, you have to meet Violet's friend. He's kinda big and scary looking, but he liked my craft!" I can't help but laugh at her description of me.

"Oh, did he? I didn't realize Violet had any friends," Nikki says, smirking at Violet while being pulled toward me by Lily.

Violet glances in my direction, an emotionless mask back on her face. "Violet's friend won't be here much longer. He's got a plane to catch, right, Viktor?" She hints at me to agree.

"Yes, I should grab my things and get going," I say, setting my cup down on the island.

"Actually, I was thinking he should stay, just until dinner. In fact, we should all go out to dinner as a family," Dante chimes in with a jester grin on his face as he looks at Violet.

She looks unimpressed with Dante's invitation. "That sounds great, but he really can't stay... Can you?" she asks, waiting for me to imply I'm busy and can't accept.

An hour ago, she wanted me to stay. Now, she's giving me the evil eye and looks ready to pounce on me if I say yes. Hmm, maybe I *should* stay.

"Actually, I don't have anything going on. I can take a later flight and stay for dinner," I say, smirking at Violet. "That is, of course, if Violet wants me to."

It might be shitty of me to throw her under the bus like this, but she's sending me mixed emotions.

"Violet would like for you to stick to your word and fu—" She stops mid-sentence when she sees Lily smiling up at her. She clears her throat and slaps on a smile. "Sure, why not?"

"Perfect! It's settled then, dinner at 7:30 sharp. Everyone be downstairs and ready by then," Dante says, picking up his daughter and leaving the kitchen. Violet glares daggers at me from across the room.

Game on, malyshka.

ONE OF MARCO'S drivers is taking us to a restaurant called Ristorante Berton. It's just Violet and I in the car together; Marco and Dante are taking their own car. Lily, unfortunately, began not feeling well, so Nikki stayed home along with Sabrina, which makes our 'family dinner' just me, Violet, and her two brothers. I'm convinced that was Dante's plan all along so they can both interrogate me more.

Violet's quiet in the car; she's been quiet all day. I spent the rest of the morning and afternoon working on my laptop in one of the guest bedrooms, talking to Dimitry about plans for a new shipment of weapons we're getting in. I didn't see Violet until later when she was dressed in a black satin dress and ready to go to dinner. She walked right by me without saying a word.

I decide it's time to break this silence. "You need to stop wearing those satin dresses, moy slomannyy angel, I'm one man. I can only control myself around you for so long."

Violet smirks at my compliment. "Who says I'm wearing this dress for you? There are plenty of fine men in Italy, maybe I'm trying to attract one of them."

I slide closer to her on the leather seat. "Careful, Violet, before I throw you over my lap and spank you for even thinking about dressing to impress another man," I growl.

She bites her lip, contemplating her next move. The car fills with tension. "We don't have time for that. Marco and Dante are already waiting at the restaurant," she says.

"Then you better behave, moy slomannyy angel," I warn her.

At least I'm not the only one trying to control their lustful urges now. I adjust myself in my seat. Great, now I'm going to be sitting at dinner with a semi-hard cock.

We arrive at dinner, and I open the car door for Violet. We walk into the restaurant and find Dante and Marco waiting for us at a table, and we take our seats. We chat about business and the cartel gang. Dante tells me how he and Nikki met, and Violet laughs and tells me all the stupid things he did to try and win her heart back. The dinner is going better than I expected. We finish our food, and another waiter brings us our dessert.

"Viktor, I wanted to ask you... How is your mother doing?" Marco asks.

"Good, she's been doing much better, thank you."

"That's good to hear," he replies.

Violet looks at us both, confused. "Was she sick?" she asks.

"She was in the hospital a few weeks ago due to a fall, but she's fine now.

That was the reason I couldn't follow through with Igor; it happened that night."

Violet looks displeased. "Why didn't you tell me?"

"I didn't think you would care."

Violet doesn't respond, she just stares at me. There's a hint of sadness in her eyes, but before I can read into it, she tucks her face away from me and picks away at her dessert. *Is she upset I didn't tell her? No, Violet wouldn't care... Would she?* I put my hand on her thigh under the table to get her attention, but she slowly moves it off without even giving me a glance.

On the drive back to the house, she doesn't say a word to me. I can't help but feel like I have fucked up somehow. When we get to the house, Marco and Dante are already there, stepping out of the car as we pull in. Once Violet and I are walking toward the front door, I grab her hand and pull her behind one of the garages. I slam her against the wall.

"Ow, Viktor, what the fuck!" she shouts.

"Why are you mad at me?" I ask her.

"I'm always mad at you," she hisses.

"Not like this. I've clearly upset you, but how?"

She sighs. "Viktor, I'm fine."

"You're good at lying, Violet."

"Thank—"

I cut her off. "But not to me, so tell me why you are upset."

"Why didn't you tell me about your mother?" she asks quietly.

Ah, I should have known. "I told you, I didn't think you cared about my personal matters."

"Well, I do," she admits. "I mean, I would care if it was something urgent about your mom. I'm not that cold-hearted, Viktor. I know we are just fucking around, but—"

I stop her. "We aren't just fucking around, *malyshka*."

A primal urge suddenly comes over me. I grab both her hands and pin them above her head with one of mine. I slide my other hand down her body, between her breast and down to her pussy.

Hiking her dress up, I find her bare. "You sat next to me at dinner with no panties on?" A mischievous smile forms on her face. I tut at her. It's a good thing I didn't play with her under the table; I would have lost my mind right there in that restaurant if I knew she wasn't wearing any panties. "Bad girl, malyshka, maybe I shouldn't give you that orgasm after all."

"Viktor, if you take your hand away from my pussy, I will fucking kill you."

"Mhm, yes, get angry, Violet, it makes it more fun when you surrender to me and melt under my touch." I move the palm of my hand in a circular motion, rubbing her clit. Violet moans loudly when I sink two fingers inside her tight, wet pussy. "Shh, be a good girl and stay quiet. You don't want your family to hear you... Or do you, malyshka? Shall I let them hear you scream my name so they all know you're mine?" She frantically shakes her head, lost in pleasure. I curl my fingers inside her, stroking her G-spot. She begins to tremble. "I want you to come all over my hand, Violet."

She moans again, biting her lip as I stroke my fingers faster. She suddenly tenses, eyes closed with her head thrown back, bucking her hips and grunting as she comes hard, her pussy clenching tight around my fingers. Fuck, I'll never get used to the sight of how beautiful she looks when she comes for me.

I pull my fingers out of her soaked, dripping pussy and bring them to my lips.

I lick her sweetness off my fingers, savoring her taste. She always tastes like sin, darkness, and fucking *mine*. Violet watches me in awe. I move my lips down to hers, less than an inch away, ready to kiss her so she can see how good she tastes when my phone rings, interrupting us. *Fuck*. I pull it out of my pocket.

"Sorry to bother you, brother," Dimitry says.

"Chto, what is it?" He sounds panicked.

"Viktor, you need to get home. Two men just tried to burn down your club! Alexi killed them before they had the chance. Idiots thought our men wouldn't spot them sneaking around the back with gas cans."

What the fuck? "Der'mo! Shut the club down for the night, I'll deal with things in the morning when I get back."

"Okay, I'll see you in the morning."

I hang up and turn back to Violet. "I have to go."

"Is everything okay?" she asks, worried.

"No, two men tried to burn down my club."

"Are you fucking serious? Well shit. I'll tell Marco, he can have the jet ready for you, it will be faster."

"Thank you, that would be great." I grab her face and give her a passionate kiss, our tastes mingling together. "We're not done here, Violet, we'll be talking about us again soon."

She nods and goes inside the house to get Marco. I want to tell her my feelings for her now, that I am falling in love with her, but it just isn't the right time. If Violet thinks she can get rid of me now, she will have a rude awakening, because I'm not going anywhere. She would have to kill me first.

CHAPTER 16

Peace in Darkness

Violet

I DROP MY bags at the door as I walk into Marco's penthouse. It's already 8:30 p.m. by the time I get in. Marco and the family decided to stay an extra two days in Italy, so I have his penthouse alone to myself until then. I may as well stop calling it Marco's and call it my own since I've been staying here more frequently after those men found my secret home and tried to kill me in it.

Now that I'm back in New York, I need to follow up with Maison to see if he found out anything about the men. When Marco's cleaning crew took care of the bodies, I got them to check and see if they had any tattoos or identification on them, but they didn't so they aren't part of the cartel. This wasn't just some random attack; those men were trained, though not very well I might add.

Speaking of attacks, I wonder how Viktor's doing with his club. I haven't spoken to him since he left after dinner last night. He texted when he was on the plane but nothing since. Maybe I should text him. I still can't believe he found me in Italy and flew all the way there because he missed me. I've never had a man go through all that trouble just to see me. My thoughts wander, thinking about Viktor when my phone rings. It's Marco. What could have possibly happened? I only just got off the plane.

"Hey, you miss me already?" I joke. "I just got to the penthouse."

"I know, I'm sorry," he says, sounding distraught. "Violet, I got a call from Derek at the Toronto Police Department." He takes a breath, steadying his voice. "They found your mother's body at her apartment—she overdosed." A cold chill runs down my spine, and my chest becomes heavy. "Her landlord found her. Looks like she had been dead for a few days," he continues. "I wanted to call as soon as I got the news, and to see what you want done with her body."

I always knew she would die alone; I told her that the very last time I saw her. "Thank you for letting me know, I don't really care what you do with the body—cremate her, bury her in an unmarked grave, I don't care," I say, bitterness lacing my tone.

Marco sighs. "Okay, I'll have her cremated, then."

"Great, I have to go. I have a few things I need to do."

"Of course, call me if you need anything," he says softly.

"I will."

I hang up and put my hand on my chest, the heavy feeling getting stronger. I have been waiting for this day to come, to be finally rid of my mother, and the last bit of my past for good. Picking my bag up off the ground, it looks like I have another flight to catch. I'm going to my childhood home for the last time.

I ARRIVED IN my hometown one hour and forty-five minutes later. An uber dropped me off around the corner from my old street where my childhood home lies. I walk through the quiet neighborhood, and all the houses still look the same. Our street was filled with old people growing up; many of them have passed away by now, and there are For Sale signs on the majority of the houses. It was a nice neighborhood back then, and the older ladies were always kind to me. They would feed me and let me inside their homes when my mother would lock me out of the house.

I now stand in front of my childhood bungalow-style home. A home filled with nothing but pain. I bought the house a year after I started working for Marco. It was my first big purchase, and I still don't really understand why I did it. I haven't been here since I bought it. The people that lived here after us didn't change much, so I kept it the way it was. The homes on either side have For Sale signs, making them vacant.

I take a deep breath and pull out the keys to the house from my pocket, then walk to the front door. An image of me sitting on the front porch alone, shivering from the cold, flashes before my eyes as I walk up the cement steps. I stick the keys in the door and turn the lock, now standing in the doorway looking into the house. I close the door behind me. Emotions I have been shoving down for years come rushing up all at once.

I make my way to the kitchen and open the cupboard by the fridge. When I bought the house, I stashed away two bottles of Vodka here, just for this occasion. I set them on the black and white vintage counter top, along with the matches I stored in the cupboard as well. The kitchen is filled with dust from no one living here in years, giving the place an eerie vibe, just like the events that went on here.

Taking one of the bottles with me and placing the matches in my back pocket, I walk past the kitchen toward my childhood bedroom, running my fingers along the door. Closing my eyes, I picture the knife marks it used to have on it from my mother trying to get into my room. The marks have been painted over and filled, but I can still feel them and hear my mother's yell echoing throughout the house.

I enter my old room, the walls still a light shade of purple, but it is empty. Taking a seat on the wooden floor, I lean against the back wall, giving me a full view of the room. Uncapping the Vodka bottle and staring at it, I think about how I haven't had a drink in five years. I stopped drinking because I needed to focus on my job. I didn't have time for hangovers or drunken mistakes. Bringing the head of the bottle to my lips, I take a sip, tilting my head back as the liquid burns my throat. Ugh, the taste is fowl, but I continue taking sips to help drown my emotions. I can see myself on this very floor with my toys, playing alone in my room while my parents yell and scream at each other outside my door.

Glancing toward the closet, I remember hiding in there from my mother when she was drunk. There's a lock on the bedroom door, but even that couldn't stop her from trying to get to me while she was having a violent episode. So I would hide in my closet with my hands on my head, covering my ears to try and block out her screaming and cursing at me. And just in case she broke in, I would leave the window open, so she would think I climbed out and left. I fell asleep in there a few times, crying myself to sleep, then by morning, she would act as though nothing happened.

She never believed what she had done to me, always accused me of lying and making things up to make her look like a bad mother. I stand up with the bottle still in hand as I walk to the closet and open it. Taking one last sip of vodka, I pour some of it inside the closet and some trailing out towards the room. Taking a few steps back, I throw the bottle in the closet, watching it shatter, each piece symbolizing how fucking broken that woman made me.

I reach into my pocket for the matches. After lighting one, I close my eyes and think about being a scared little girl, cowering, afraid of her own mother. I open my eyes, staring at the flame and angrily throw the match into the closet. Fire immediately ignites as I turn to leave the room, letting the closet and the memories burn.

Walking back to the kitchen, I stop short, turning my head to the right where my mother's bedroom used to be. Past memories of her laying in bed, covered in vomit and god knows what else, haunt me where I stand. *Fuck that, I can't go in there.* I have had enough flashback memories. Stomping into the kitchen, I grab the other bottle off the counter and throw it at the wall, screaming. It shatters, liquid and glass clinging to the wall and floor. I light another match—*fuck this house! I should've burned it down when I bought it,* I think to myself and throw the match onto the spilled vodka.

I go to the side door that leads to the backyard; my childhood swing set still stands, but the wood is rotting, and the green plastic covering on the swing is torn off, exposing more of the chain. The metal shed in the back by the gate has seen better days. The doors are rusted shut, so I have to kick them in order to get them open. Once they do, I grab the gas canisters I left here and start pouring gasoline all over the back of the house. My nostrils burn with the strong smell of the gas.

Once the canister is empty, I toss it back into the shed, grabbing the other one. My phone vibrates in my pocket several times, but I ignore it, moving to the other side of the house and pouring more gas on it. I light my final match and throw it, watching it bounce off the brick wall and land in a pool of gasoline, setting it aflame. I walk back over to the swing set and sit down on one of the swings, watching the house go up in smoke. I let out the breath I've been holding since I got here, the heavy weight on my chest disappearing.

When the flames start to grow higher, I get off the swing and walk over to the gate, exiting the backyard. My phone vibrates again, but I hardly feel it this time. Enraptured by the flames engulfing my childhood home, taking what's left of my past and burning it to ash.

"Goodbye, Mom."

CHAPTER 17

Moy Slomannyy Angel
My Broken Angel

Viktor

I WAIT FOR Violet in Marco's penthouse. His guards let me in without question once I told them who I was; they called Marco to confirm it was okay. I tried asking him myself where Violet was, like last time when she wasn't answering me, but he told me he couldn't help me and to just leave her alone for today. I was pissed; I wasn't buying that she was fine.

Something is wrong with Violet. I can feel it in my soul. I have been here waiting for almost three hours, either in this chair or pacing the penthouse. It's now 12:30 a.m. and still no sign of her. I'm used to Violet's snarky comments and her getting angry with me, but she's never ignored my calls before. I swear to god and the devil himself, if something happened to her, I will tear this fucking city apart and everyone in it to find who's responsible. As I sit in my angry stupor, the penthouse front door opens. Violet walks in, looking absolutely wrecked.

I jump up from my seat. "Violet!" I yell.

She turns her head in my direction. "I don't have the energy for you, Viktor, so if you're here to fuck or fight, come back another time," she says, her voice weak with exhaustion.

"Where did you go? You have been gone all night. I tried calling to see if you were okay, but you ignored all my calls," I say to her.

"Stop with the relationship, where-were-you bullshit right now, Viktor, I need sleep," she snaps, taking off her boots.

"Violet, what happened?" I ask, concerned. I get closer to her, smelling smoke. *What the fuck is going on, where did she come from, smelling like smoke?*

Violet sighs. "If you must know, Viktor, my mother died. I burned down my childhood home in Toronto, and I'm extremely exhausted from the events and my flight. There, you're all up to date now," she says nonchalantly, moving past me toward the bedroom. I grab her arm, stopping her. "What?" she snaps, then tries to push me away.

"Violet, stop! You're not going anywhere, why didn't you call me?"

"Because I didn't think you cared about my personal life," she spits, throwing my words back at me. "And besides, it's not a big deal, I hated my mother. I told you that."

"But you never explained why, and when I try to ask, you shut me out."

"Fine! You want to know about my mother, my childhood so badly?" she shouts, storming over to a painting hanging on the far wall in the living room. She lifts the painting up off the wall, exposing a safe hiding behind it. Violet punches in a code on the keypad, and the safe opens. She reaches in and pulls out two books. Walking back toward me, she throws them onto the coffee table. "There you go, enjoy. And for the last time, I'm going to bed!"

Violet walks away from me and toward her room. The door slams shut behind her, leaving me alone. I glance at the books on the table; one looks to be a journal, the other a photo album. Taking a seat on the couch, I open the album up first, flipping it to the first page. A photo of a little red-headed girl with a wide smile catches my attention. I can tell right away it's Violet. It's weird seeing her look so young and happy, innocent even. It's also hard to imagine her as anything but the ruthless woman she is today. She was clearly a silly kid, I think, smiling at the image.

My stomach sinks when I flip to the next page; things might not look as happy as they seem. There's another photo on the same page of a brunette woman in a hospital bed, with a sleeping baby in her arms. This must be

Violet's mother. Violet looks nothing like her, which I'm sure she's probably grateful for. Her mother is smiling down at baby Violet in her arms, and a cold chill runs through my body as I flip to the next page. Intense rage engulfs me.

Photos of a young Violet looking no more than maybe seven or eight, is wearing a hospital gown. Her arms and legs are covered in bruises, and she looks scared. The happy girl from the first photo has disappeared—who hurt her? Was it her mother? Her father? She never really spoke ill of him, just that he was an alcoholic, but she didn't sound angry when saying it.

I close the photo album, seeing enough for now and pick up the journal. She must have been carrying this journal around for years, the edges torn, and it has a musty smell to it. The first journal entry dates back to 2009, which would make Violet about twelve years old writing this. The writing is messy, each pen stroke looking as if she was pushing on the pen too hard. There's a water stain at the bottom of the page, and I can't help but wonder if she was crying. My chest aches above my heart as I start to read her entry.

April 16 2009

Why does she hate me so much? I don't understand, I didn't do anything wrong. Mom chased me to my room with a knife. She keeps banging on my door and yelling at me. I can't leave! She said she was going to kill me. How could she want to kill me? I'm her daughter. I'm so scared, I ran into my closet and tried to grab the phone, but she unplugged it from the wall. Why won't she just stop? She keeps screaming "I'm going to kill you!" I just want her to stop.

My fingers dig into the journal, ready to tear it to shreds. This woman is lucky she's already dead, or I would be killing her myself for causing not only her own daughter this much pain, but a child. How could she try to kill Violet? I don't understand what could have made her mother so angry that she would choose to do something like that. And where was her father when this happened? I turn to the next page, hoping for answers.

March 5 2013

I'm done with my mother! I never want to see her again! She embarrassed me in front of my friends for the last time! She called me a slut at my sweet 16 birthday party in front of everyone! She was feeding wine to my friends like it was water, getting them drunk, it was humiliating! I hate her! I just want a normal mom. Why can't I have one that loves me?

Jesus Christ. I couldn't imagine being a teen girl and having your mother do that, and on her birthday. I doubt Violet ever celebrated her birthday after that. What the hell is wrong with this woman? The next page is dated for that same year.

September 8 2013

I left my mom's house late last night. I heard her talking with a man outside my bedroom door. I'm so tired of her bringing random men home from the bar, it's gross and creepy. I heard them talking about me, the man asked how much it would be for me and I didn't understand what they were talking about. It creeped me out so I left and went to my dad's. I don't know how long I'll be here but I don't want to go back there. I need to start realizing that she will never be a good mom and she will never love me.

I'm about ready to throw this book across the fucking room! If that son of a bitch got a hold of Violet... No, I can't think about that. My body can't physically handle the thought. If he did, I will kill every fucking man her mother was ever with until I find him. Her mother was an evil woman; I'm glad Violet is rid of her, but I know these memories will still haunt her even though she's gone. The last entry is dated 2019. I'm hoping maybe twenty-one-year-old Violet had something good happen in her life. Reading the first line, all hope I had for her vanishes.

May 4 2019

Why does no man want me? They want me maybe for a day, a few weeks but then they leave. They move on to the woman they really want and it's never me. Am I so incapable of being loved that no guy will ever want me? No guy I've dated has ever wanted to even try to be in a relationship with me, build a life with me... A future. Everyone around me keeps saying I'm young and not to worry, that the right man will find me and I'm sick of hearing it. They don't understand what it's like to feel so unwanted. If no man wants me now then what hope should I have for when I'm older? All my relationships so far have failed. I don't understand, I give and I give. I love them with all my heart but it's never enough. I'm never enough.

My heart shatters seeing Violet speak so little of herself. The guys she's dated in her past were not real men; they were boys who were too stupid and blind to see the amazing woman they had in front of them. Too scared to deal with her past and the demons that come with it.

I slam the book closed and am on my feet in seconds, heading to her bedroom. I quietly open the door, trying not to wake her. I walk over to her bed, to the side where she sleeps and sit on the edge of the mattress. Violet is sleeping on her side, and I gently brush away a few hairs covering her face, running two fingers along her soft cheek. Even fast asleep, she still looks stressed.

I sit there watching her while whispering sweet words to her in Russian. "Yesli by ya mog zabrat' vsyu bol', kotoruyu ty chuvstvuyesh', i vernut' yeye sebe, ya by eto sdelal. Ty slishkom dolgo zashchishchala svoi chuvstva i okhranyala svoye serdtse v odinochku. Teper' ya budu tvoim zashchitnikom, Vayolet. Ty v bezopasnosti, moy slomannyy angel."

If I could take all the pain you feel away and into me, I would. You have protected your feelings and guarded your heart alone for too long. I will be your protector now, Violet. You are safe, my broken angel.

CHAPTER 18

Trust

Violet

I'M WOKEN BY rough hands, softly caressing my thighs, working their way up my body and wrapping around my waist.

"Good morning, moy slomannyy angel," Viktor groans.

"Mhm," I moan back, still feeling tired from last night. Viktor pulls my body closer to him, and my ass hits his front. His hard cock presses against my ass cheek. "Viktor, about last night…" I start, remembering that Viktor read my journal, exposing my past and baring all my internal wounds to him.

"Shh, we'll talk after," he whispers in my ear.

"After what?" I ask.

He grinds his cock against my ass, while massaging my thighs. I moan into his touch, his rough, manly hands feeling amazing on my skin.

"After I fuck you and make you come a few times, then we'll talk," he rasps.

"A few? I think you're letting your ego go to your head again," I tease him.

Viktor bites my shoulder playfully. "Don't underestimate my abilities when it comes to your body, malyshka, or I'll tie you to this bed and not let you leave until you beg me to make you stop coming."

"That's a horrible threat ,Viktor, I expected better from you."

He wraps his hand around my throat. "Don't tease me, Violet, I had a plan to wake you up nicely with my cock deep inside your pussy, but I can change that and just fuck your sassy mouth again," he threatens.

As much as I love teasing him and the feel of his cock in my mouth,

Viktor and I haven't had sex since the night at his place. When he was a fucking beast and almost shattered his entire glass shower just to get to me. Since then, my pussy has felt empty, repeating the feeling of him inside me for the first time over and over again. I push my ass closer to him, moving my hips slightly to show him what I want.

He chuckles. "Nice try, malyshka, but this time, if you want my cock, you're going to have to ask for it."

"Fat chance," I tease.

He continues to massage my thighs. Getting closer to my pussy each time but not going any higher. His hands move to my ass, kneading my muscles. Fuck, this is torture. What he's doing feels nice—better than nice—but it's not what I want. Viktor turns his attention to my breasts next, massaging each one and tweaking my nipples, too gently.

"Still not breaking yet?" he whispers.

I shake my head, and he shifts around behind me. When he gets back into position, his bare cock is between my ass cheeks. I'm only wearing underwear and a T-shirt, and my panties do nothing to stop the feel of his cock head nudging at my entrance. Oh god, he's so close to being inside me. If he just moved my panties to the side, he could slip inside me easily, giving us both what we need right now. Maybe if I shift a little, I could do it myself without him noticing.

I try to move, but Viktor grabs my hips, halting me. "It's not happening, Violet, not until you beg."

""You like it when I beg, don't you?" I say seductively, trying to get him to be the one who caves first. I slide my hand down to my pussy, rubbing it and collecting some of my arousal on my fingers.

"Violet..." Viktor warns, watching me bring my fingers up to his mouth.

"Look how wet I am for you, Viktor."

He grabs my fingers and brings them to his mouth, sucking them clean.

Great. That was supposed to make him surrender, not turn me on even more.

"Mm, you do taste delicious, malyshka, but again... Nice try." He smirks. "You may as well just end both our suffering and beg," Viktor says, rubbing his cock against the seam of my panties. I moan. "That's it, keep moaning for me, Violet, doesn't my cock feel good?"

I bite my lip, trying to stop myself from moaning again. Viktor starts kissing my neck. *Fuck! I can't take it!* I'm five seconds from cracking and begging this man to fuck me into this mattress. He pulls my panties to the side and rubs his cock on my bare pussy, the tip rubbing against my clit.

I break. "Stop teasing me and fuck me already, Viktor! Please!"

He chuckles. "Good girl."

He rips my panties clean off and thrusts his cock deep inside me, stretching my pussy around his girth. His thrusts are slow and gentle, not anything like the first time he fucked me. I enjoy rough sex—it's one of my kinks—but the way Viktor's fucking me slow and deep is euphoric. It's somehow more intimate, the way he's holding me while he fucks me makes me feel like I'm precious to him.

"Fuck, you feel good, let's start with orgasm one," he rasps, snaking a hand down to my pussy and rubbing my clit.

Viktor's other hand wraps back around my throat as his thrusts become faster. I lift my left leg on top of his, letting him go deeper. He puts more pressure on my clit, and my orgasm is brewing quickly. Viktor seems to never have a hard time making me come. I was joking with him earlier; he may have a big ego, but it's justified.

"I can feel you're close, Violet, mm I can't wait to feel your pussy tighten around my cock," he growls. His words make me want to come faster for him. Hearing him get pleasure from giving it to me is one of the sexiest things he does. I could come just from the sound of his voice, telling me how much he loves fucking me. "Come for me, Violet, I want to feel you come on my cock."

I moan loudly, a rush of pleasure flooding through my body, clenching my abdomen and my pussy as I come. My vision becomes fuzzy, and my body twitches from the aftershocks of my climax.

Viktor sucks in a breath through his teeth. "Fucking perfect, that was only one. I told you I would give you a few, so I'm nowhere near done with you yet."

Viktor rolls on top of me, his lips grazing mine before he grabs my jaw, tilting my head up to meet him in a fearsome kiss. Viktor breaks the kiss and pulls his cock out of me. I whine in protest, but before I can complain, he throws my legs up in the air and pushes my knees to my chest , spreading me open wide for him. He feasts on my pussy like I've been starving him of tasting me for days. He suctions his mouth around my clit, and I scream, wreathing beneath him, coming hard for the second time.

"That's two. One more for me, moy slomannyy angel," he demands.

"I-I can't," I say, breathless with lust.

"I wasn't asking, Violet, you're going to come for me one last time, then I'll fill your needy little pussy with my cum."

With a gleam in his eyes, he lifts my legs on top of his shoulders. Then he slides himself back inside me, raises my hips up, hitting my G-spot over and over again. The bedroom fills with the sounds of skin on skin, and I close my eyes, getting lost in my pleasure. Viktor nips at my ankle, causing me to open my eyes.

"Don't close your eyes, you look at me when you fall apart for me," he says, moving his hips faster.

"Fuck, Viktor!" I cry out.

His gaze travels down my entire body and back up again. "That's it, Violet, take my cock, take it like the filthy little thing you are." His words, this angle, it's too much. I come for the third time with a silent scream. *"Fuck!"* Viktor roars, emptying his seed inside me.

My body is numb from all my orgasms as Viktor gently pulls out his cock, some of his release spilling out of me along with it. I could pass out right now; I just might, actually. Viktor leaves the bedroom and goes to my ensuite washroom, then the water starts running, but I'm too tired to move.

Viktor comes back into the room. "Come on, moy slomannyy angel, let's take a nice hot bath," he says, gently kissing my cheek.

I whine, turning onto my side. My body feels like jello. "Too tired."

Viktor laughs, lifting me up and carrying me to the bathroom. This man sure does love to carry me, I don't think I've ever walked to a bathroom myself with him. He sets me down on the counter top, the cool stone feeling nice on my still-heated skin. Viktor pours some bubble bath into the tub. I watch him as I think back to a question that's been left on my mind.

"I've been meaning to ask you, what does 'moy slomannyy angel' mean? You keep calling me that, why?" I ask.

Viktor sets the bubble bath down on the counter and turns his full attention toward me. "It means 'my broken angel,'" he says sweetly, and my heart sinks, ready to freeze up again.

"Are you joking? That's what you have been calling me this whole time, a fucking broken angel?" I yell. "That's what you think of me? As a broken woman that needs a big strong man to save her? Fuck you, Viktor!" I snap at him, ready to hop off this counter and stab him.

That permanent smirk he always wears vanishes. "If you calm down for just a minute, I will tell you why." Reluctantly, I look at him. "I call you my broken angel, one, because you're mine, and two, it's not because I see you as weak or fragile. You may be broken deep down, but you feed off it. Instead of letting the hurt, the pain of your past consume you, you use it as a weapon, a way to both destroy and protect. Much like an angel would, and I admire you for that. That's why I call you 'moy slomannyy angel.' You're an amazing woman, and the fact that you don't see that pisses me off. But I'm not pissed at you, I'm pissed at the people who have influenced you into thinking for years that was the fucking truth."

I stare at him, lost for words. I'm conflicted. On one hand, I'm still upset that he calls me broken, but the fact that he sees it as a strength of mine has made it less hurtful. In his eyes, I'm this amazing woman who just can't seem to see herself, and maybe he's right. Maybe the people from my past had a huge impact on that. I wish I could see what he sees, even just for a second.

Viktor turns off the tap. "The bath's ready."

I hop off the counter as he holds out his hand for me to take. His big hand engulfs mine as he guides me into the tub, the hot water burning my feet when I first step in, then turns to a relaxing warmth as I submerge the rest of my body. Viktor just stands there, watching me.

"Are you not joining me?" I ask.

"Do you want me to?" he replies.

"Yes."

I'm not one for cuddling, but I just need him close to me right now. Viktor removes his black briefs. I try not to be a weirdo and stare at his cock for too long as he climbs into the tub. The fact I take one look at it and my body's reaction is to either open my legs or my mouth for him is a little insane. I guess that's what good dick will do to a girl. The tub is a big claw foot tub, but Viktor's broad shoulders make it look smaller than it is. God, he's so hot, it's hard to look at him right now, and my body is screaming at me not to ask for a round two.

"This won't work, you're too far away from me. I need you closer." He spreads his legs out, his knees now above the water.

He beckons me closer to him. "Come here, Violet."

I smile at him and move awkwardly toward him, creating sudsy waves as I get closer. On my knees in front of his spread legs, he gestures to me with his finger to turn around. I roll my eyes at him and turn my body, my back now facing him. He pulls me closer so my back is flush against his muscular chest, and wraps his arms around my waist. I settle into him, resting my head against his shoulder. His chest rises and falls against my back as he breathes, the sensation comforting me.

"Close enough for you?" I joke.

"No, but in this tiny tub, it will do."

I laugh. "The tub's not tiny, you're just a beast." I shift, trying to get my lower back more comfortable, when my butt bumps into Viktor's cock.

"Don't move so much, malyshka, you will make me hard again, and we both know your body can't handle me again so soon," he rasps. He's right; I'm still sore from that last position he put me in. Pretty sure he was hitting my G-spot and my ovaries all in one thrust. "And I said after I was done making you come a few times, we would talk." Damn, I was hoping he forgot about that. "Let's start with the journal."

I sigh. Well, he's already read it; he knows about my darkness already, so there's no point in hiding anything else from him. "I started journaling to try and help get my thoughts out of my head, to hopefully quiet some of the demons my mother put in there, and to keep a record of the things she did in case anything were to happen to me," I tell him.

"The man that asked if he could—" He stops mid-sentence and doesn't finish his thought, like he can't say it. I know exactly who he's talking about, so I don't need him to. "What happened to him? He never found you, did he?" he asks, sounding pained.

"No, I never went back to her house after that. I lived with my dad until I met Marco. I tried to find him, but I never saw his face, just heard his voice, and since I wasn't in contact with my mother, it wasn't enough to go on. So the man that wanted to buy me is still out there," I explain, pissed that I was too young at the time to be able to do anything about him.

Viktor holds me tighter, sensing my anger. "Where was your father when this happened?"

"Jail. My mother put him there, she had a restraining order against him. There wasn't anything he could do, really."

"Violet, I know saying I'm sorry for what happened to you probably means nothing, but I am. I'm sorry for the little girl in you that got robbed of her childhood."

"Thank you," I say softly. He kisses my shoulder as another piece of my cold heart melts away. I trace my finger along his bicep, across the scar I gave him. *Should I apologize for that now?* Nah, at the time, he did deserve it. "Since we're on the topic of children, why did you get a vasectomy? Don't you need an heir or someone blood-related to take your place when you retire, or if something happens to you?" I couldn't say the word "die" out loud; thinking of Viktor dying makes me physically ill now.

"No, I have Dimitry for that. He's next to take my place when the time comes. As for the reason I got one, it was because I never really saw myself as a father, and I didn't want to have to train my child to be like me, like my father did. What about you? Why don't you want children?"

"Same as you, kinda, I never saw myself as a mother, and I was afraid of becoming my mother. Her bipolar disorder, her drinking, all started after she had me. I was afraid I would be the same."

"I understand, but just so you know, you would make a good mother, Violet. I saw how you were with Lily; you could never do the things your mother did to you, to her or any child." He placed a kiss on my head. "I get why you decided to work for Marco, you have done well saving women, but don't you think maybe it's time someone saved you? That someone took care of and protected you?"

"I don't need a man to take care of me," I huffed.

"You're taking my words the wrong way, Violet. I know you don't need a man to take care of you, but you should have one. I'm not a perfect man, Violet."

"Viktor—" I try to stop him.

"Just listen. You can't deny the feelings we have for each other, and I know you're scared of getting hurt again, but I could be a good man to you, Violet," he says, sounding so honest.

"I'm not saying you wouldn't be, Viktor. The problem is, I don't think I could give you the same in return, and that would break me," I confess, exposing more of my heart to him. My phone rings on the counter, and I reach for it, shaking my hands free of water before grabbing it. "Hello?" I answer.

"Hey, it's Maison. You're not gonna believe this, sunshine, but I found that cartel gang's hide out! I'll send you the deets of where it's located. I think there might be women being held there for trafficking, I was going to go check the place out."

"No! Do not go there alone, it's too dangerous. Wait for me, send me the address and I'll meet you there later tonight, after I tell Marco."

"Sounds good, boss, I'll wait for your call." We both hang up.

"Who was that?" Viktor asks.

"That was Maison, he found the cartel gang's location. I need to call Marco."

"It can wait."

"What? No, I need to call him now!"

Viktor grabs my waist and pulls me back to him. I squeal, throwing my phone quickly and it lands on the bathmat. "In a bit, I'm not done with your body yet."

CHAPTER 19

The Hunter Becomes The Hunted

Violet

VIKTOR AND I are on our way to meet with Marco and Dante at Marco's office. He just flew in this morning, and I told him to go straight there to meet us. We spent the rest of the morning fucking and talking about our lives, and Viktor told me about his parents and his mom's condition. It was the best morning I think I've had in a long time, just talking about life while wrapped in his arms. I was able to forget about all the bad things; my darkness was temporarily at bay with him, as it always is.

We walk inside Marco's office, and Dante and Marco are already sitting down, waiting as we enter.

"Hey! I have news. Maison found the cartel's hideout," I say, direct and to the point. I'm not willing to waste time. I need to get to that cabin before the girls are gone.

"Way to go, Maison, finally stepping up his game," Dante says.

"That's great, we're going to need it. I just got a call before you walked in. The leader of the gang wants to meet tonight. He said he would like to negotiate a peace treaty and sounded genuine, but I'm going to bring extra men with us just in case," Marco announces.

"That's perfect, you guys can go to the meeting while I go check out this cabin. Maison mentioned they could be holding girls hostage there for trafficking. I can save them and meet you guys back here after the meeting," I say quickly.

"We will meet them here. You aren't going to that cabin alone, Violet,"

Viktor states sternly.

"Yes, I am, I'll be fine. Maison will meet me there. You need to go with the guys to the meeting, it's important, and don't forget they stole from you, too. You're at war with them just as much as we are. I promise I will send you the address so you know exactly where I am," I explain, trying to keep him calm.

"Fine, but if anything goes wrong, you call me right away, understood?" Viktor gives me a threatening look.

I smirk back at him. "Yes, beast, I understand." I appreciate his concern for me, but it isn't necessary.

"Just be careful, Red, these guys are scum, and we don't know if all his men will be at the meeting. If there's girls there, he will have men guarding them," Dante says.

"I know, you all act like this is my first heist. I'll be fine, stop worrying."

I turn to leave them, and Viktor follows behind, stopping me when I'm halfway out the door. "I don't like this, Violet." He looks at me, troubled.

"Viktor, I have done this many times, please stop worrying about me and just trust me."

He sighs. "Okay, but you better call me."

"I will."

"I mean it, malyshka, or I'll hunt you down and punish you with my cock in front of all those men before I kill them."

My body fills with excitement at his threat. "Again, your threats stink," I tease, standing on my tippy toes to kiss him on the cheek. I run away before he has a chance to change his mind and lock me in Marco's office. "Good luck at the meeting!" I yell, waving goodbye and heading back to the car.

The cabin is in a remote location, about two hours from where I am now. I shoot Maison a text to tell him to leave now. He didn't say how many girls might be there, but I plan on getting them all the hell out of there and killing anyone who stands in my way.

THIS OLD, ABANDONED cabin smells like garbage. That's not an exaggeration, garbage that's been sitting out all day in the hot sun, and I can see why. There's trash everywhere—open food wrappers, cans of energy drinks, moldy food stuck to plates. These must be left from the cartel gang; they don't usually feed the women and young girls. They drug them and give them water, but that's about it. There's no other signs of any guards in here yet. *Where the hell are they?* I wasn't exactly subtle entering the place; if anyone was here, they would have all tried to shoot me by now.

There's no way they all went to the meeting and left the girls here, unless there never was any to begin with, or I'm too late and they already took them to a different location to be sold. *Fuck, I hope I'm not too late.* I keep searching the cabin, it's not big so it doesn't take me long. There's not much to this place, and there's some documents on a table in what I think is the living room area. There's no couches, or any other seating, just the one chair by the table.

I start to go through some of the papers, stopping when I see an orange folder. I open it, the contents shocking me—photos of Viktor and me. There's two photos of us leaving the restaurant the night he requested the favor. My body shudders, and my forehead creases in confusion as I stare at a photo of us that had to be taken through Marco's penthouse bathroom window. It would have been taken this morning. In the photo, Viktor and I are in the bathtub. I'm straddling his hips with a look of utter bliss on my face. *What the fuck?* Why the hell would they take this? There's a few photos of the outside of Marco's warehouse, but that's it. Most of them are either

Viktor and me, or just me. What's their obsession with me? Are they trying to get to me so they can use me as bait to get to Marco and Viktor?

So many questions run through my mind as I rummage through the papers on the table looking for answers. I find a document that catches my eye. It has the address of where the meeting is with the cartel, but there's something strange written at the bottom of the page. It says *The timer goes off*. Timer? Timer for what? None of this is making any sense. Where are the girls? Why are there so many stalker photos of only Viktor and me, and not Dante or Marco? Shouldn't the cartel have been watching them, too?

Frustrated, I start pushing papers around, throwing the ones that are useless to me on the ground. In my haste, I stop, finding a paper with a diagram on it. I examine the image, trying to understand what exactly it is I'm looking at, when I realize it's not just an ordinary diagram. It's instructions on how to make a fucking bomb. I start putting two and two together, and realize that the timer for the meeting location means that's when the bomb will go off. *It's a setup!* There's no peace treaty meeting; it was all a lie to lure them there so the cartel could get rid of them all easily. I grab my phone and run outside, dialing Viktor's number.

"Hello, moy—"

I cut him off. "Viktor! It's a setup!" I yell.

"What?!" he asks.

"Don't go to the meeting, turn the car around, now! The whole thing is a setup, they are planning on blowing you guys up!" I explain.

"Shit!" Viktor talks to Marco and the others in the background. "Tell the men to turn the car around!" he shouts at them.

"What? Why?" Marco says.

"Violet said it's a trap, they are planning on killing us all."

"Motherfuckers," Dante curses.

"Where are you now?" Viktor asks me.

"I'm still at the cabin. Viktor, there's more to it. I don't know what's going on, but—"

I stop talking, the hairs on the back of my neck standing up as I sense someone standing behind me. Before I have time to grab my knife, a sharp pain pierces through my neck. I'm put in a headlock, still gripping my phone as I struggle to get out of the person's hold.

"Hello, sunshine," is the last thing I hear before I'm let go, dropping my phone, my body hitting the ground along with it. My head hits the pavement as I'm met with darkness.

CHAPTER 20

Note to Self:

Keep Your Friends and Your Enemies in the Same Category

Violet

WELL, THAT WAS unexpected. I did not see this coming. Of all the men to hate me and want me dead, Maison would have been way at the bottom of my list. I can't believe I didn't put it together sooner. The question is why? Why is he doing this? Was I that bad of a boss, he wants me dead? My body is numb. Whatever drug he gave me courses through my veins. I can't move, just my head which aches. I open my eyes weakly, and Maison is hovering above me, smiling.

"Wakey wakey, Violet," he mocks.

"What did you give me?" I ask, my voice cracking. Speaking takes so much strength.

"A muscle relaxant. It weakens your muscles. You can try and move them, but your limbs will feel like you're lifting thousand-ton weights. I didn't give you a high dosage, just enough to make you temporarily weak so you're defenseless against me, but still able to feel every ounce of pain I will be inflicting on you," he spews.

"I'm a little surprised, Maison, I thought you were better than this," I snap.

"You don't know a fucking thing about me, Violet! But you could have, if you weren't such a selfish bitch, this all could have been avoided," he says venomously.

"What the fuck are you talking about? I didn't do shit to you, Maison.

Marco and I gave you a job, we gave you a purpose in life instead of living on the streets," I try to yell, but my voice is still hoarse from the drug.

"You made me your fucking lackey! You bossed me around, made me run stupid errands for you, and not once did you ever see me as anything else but your servant!" he shouts. "So I decided to take matters into my own hands. I was only going to start with little things to get back at you, like fucking with the lives of the people closest to you. I started off with Marco's shipment, leaking the warehouse's information to the cartel. I was going to pin the whole thing on you, send the information to them through your phone so it looked like you betrayed him. It was simple, he would have taken you out of the family, and you would no longer be my boss and have no one to care for you but me. But then, you chose to fuck that Russian instead of me!" he spits.

Holy fuck, Maison is more delusional than I thought.

I let out a burst of enraged laughter. "That's what this is all about? You're mad because I wouldn't fuck you?" I continue to laugh at him. "You're fucking pathetic."

Maison kicks me in the ribs. *Fuck!* I bite through the pain; it's all I can do since I can't move to defend myself. I need to stall him as much as possible, even if I make him more angry doing so. If what he said was true about the drug he gave me, that means the low dosage shouldn't last long. I just need to stall him until I can move at least one hand to get my knife.

"You're calling me pathetic, but you're the one laying on the ground helpless."

"Yeah, because you drugged me. You had to paralyze me because you know you can't fight me without it." I laugh right in his face. "That's why I never fucked you. I like real men, not little boys who pretend to be them."

Maison pulls my hair, getting right in my face. "I could fuck you right now if I wanted to, you're weak enough. It would be easy, but you're not even worth that to me anymore," he says, slamming my face back to the ground. The cement slices across my face, burning my skin. "I wasn't planning on you calling Viktor so quickly, but that's okay, I have backup plans for a reason. The bomb will still go off, killing the cartel. It's amazing what you can learn on the internet and the voice changing apps you can use. I pretended to be the leader of both groups, calling the cartel and saying the Italians wanted to make a truce and vice versa. Then all I had to do was call you and convince you that they were hiding girls here. I knew you would come running. This place isn't even the cartel's, I found this abandoned cabin for sale on Craigslist." He laughs. "Once the bomb goes off, the members that didn't go to the meeting will blame the Italians for it, creating an even bigger war between them," he states.

"Viktor knows I'm here. If I don't get a chance to kill you, he will, along with Marco and Dante."

He thinks he has everything figured out, but even if I don't make it, Maison will never be free. They will all hunt him down and slaughter him in the most brutal way.

Maison crouches down beside me. "Come on, Violet, when are you gonna learn they don't give a shit about you? Marco only needs you for killing, but he can always train someone else to take your place. And Viktor... Well, I'm sure we both know what he's using you for. All you're good for is killing and fucking, that's it, Violet."

He's trying to get under my skin, but he can't; I won't let him. "Fuck you, Maison!" I seethe.

"We talked about that already, I'm not interested. On the off chance they decide to come save you, I set up tire spikes along the road that leads here, so they won't make it to you in time. By the time they find another way here, get another car, you'll be dead," he says with a sinister smile.

There's no way Maison is doing all this just because I rejected him.

There's more to this plan than he's letting on. "I get why you want me and the cartel dead, but why Marco? He saved you, Maison."

His nostrils flare. "He should have saved my mother! He could have saved her, but he chose his own life instead!"

My eyes squint in confusion. "What are you talking about? Your mother was dead when he got there."

"No, she wasn't! That night, he and his men came in, guns blazing. If they had come in quietly, without notice, she would still be alive, but he was selfish and didn't think of that. All he cared about was killing the cartel, and as soon as the leader heard them coming, they started shooting women. My mother was one of them," he clarifies.

Even if what he's saying is true, Marco wouldn't have known that. It was all an accident, but Maison is a psychopath who can't see that.

"How do you know all that?" I ask.

"Because I found the ones that survived, and they told me everything. That's why I want him dead."

Everything starts clicking together. "You found my house, you sent those men."

That sinister grin reappears. "Of course I did. I hired them to kidnap you, they were supposed to bring you to me. So that I could finish you off. I thought at least one of them would survive, but this is why you can't rely on other people to do your dirty work for you, can you, Violet?"

His grin deepens. His words fuel more anger in me. I should have killed him the very first time he ever called me sunshine, but Maison was good at hiding his true nature. I failed myself with him.

My phone dings, distracting us both from our heated conversation. Maison turns to it and picks it up off the ground. All I can do is watch him. He has an evil grin on his face as he pulls out a switchblade from his pocket. He grabs my face, squeezing it roughly and brings the knife's blade against my cheek.

"How about we give your little Russian lover a call, let him hear that he's not the only man that can make you scream."

CHAPTER 21

Betrayal

Viktor

I'VE TRIED CALLING Violet back several times and texting her, but still no answer.

"I can't get hold of Violet," I say out loud. Marco and Dante are in the car with me, heading to the cabin where Violet is.

"She's probably fine, if you heard Maison's voice in the background then that means she's safe with him. He might have just snuck up on her and she dropped her phone. He's always doing dumb shit like that to mess with her," Dante reassures me.

"Maybe, how much longer until we're there?" I call out to the driver.

"Twenty minutes," he responds.

Fuck, I'm getting more antsy by the minute. I wish she would at least send a text to calm my nerves. When she first called me, panicked about the bomb, the worry in her voice was clear, and it made my heart burn for her. Knowing she cares for my safety just as much as I do hers, but she still sounded scared even when I mentioned we were turning around.

I'm getting that same feeling in my gut that something's not right, like I did the night Violet's mom died. Maison called her sunshine in the background, and it made my blood boil. Not just because he called my woman sunshine, which no man should ever call her if they expect to live afterward, and everyone says it's innocent, but the way he said it didn't sound like a friendly welcome. Then shortly after, the phone cut out, and she was gone.

I will say it was hard to believe her at first when she said the whole thing was a setup. It's a hell of a risk for the cartel to take out both Mafia families without serious backlash. My family and Marco's would both be after them, and having both the Italians and Russians hunting them down wouldn't be survivable. Dimitry would avenge me and make sure there would be no cartel member left alive to tell the tale.

I check my phone again; I'm more than just worried about Violet. If she only dropped it, she would have found another way to call me back. Maybe I should try her one more time. Just then, the car skids, and we almost veer off the road. The car behind us with our men in it does the same.

"What the fuck was that?!" Dante yells.

We all jump out of the vehicle to see what the fuck made us stop, observing the road ahead and our surroundings. Dante and I both look down at the car's tires which are completely flat. I curse in Russian.

"How did this happen?" I yell.

Marco bends down and picks something up off the road. "This," he says, showing us a tire spike. "The road's covered with them."

My stomach sinks. "Someone obviously didn't want us getting to that cabin," I say.

"Did the cartel do this? To stop people from finding the place?" Dante asks.

"No, these couldn't have been here long, or Violet and Maison wouldn't have been able to get there; these spikes would have been placed here after," I explain to him. "Call your men, Marco, see if they can find another road that goes there." He nods and picks up his phone to call them. I turn to one of my men. "Do the same," I order.

"Da, Packhan," he says, leaving us.

While we are trying to figure out what the fuck to do next, my phone finally rings with Violet's name. *Thank fuck.*

"Are you okay, malyshka?" I ask her. I hear nothing but movement.

"Hello? Violet?" I yell her name into the phone.

"Viktor!" She calls my name, but her voice is faint, sounding weak with pain.

"Violet! Are you okay? What's wrong?" The next sound out of her mouth is a blood-curdling scream. "Violet!" I yell, as if yelling her name might help her when I know it can't. "Violet, I'm coming! I'm coming for you, moy slomannyy angel." She doesn't respond, and instead, there's a man's laughter, then the call disconnects. "*Fuck!*" I yell, smashing my phone on the ground, the screen shattering. I run my fingers through my hair, pulling at the roots in anger.

"What's going on? What's wrong with Violet?" Dante yells at me, but I ignore him.

Blood fills my ears; all I can hear is the sound of my pulse pounding. Violet's scream plays in my head. *You need to get to her, Viktor, just get to her.* I don't think any longer, I just run. Dante and Marco's faint voices shout behind me, then their footsteps follow suit.

I stay along the curb, closer to the grass to avoid the tire spikes. The last thing I need is one through the foot preventing me from running. Who am I kidding, not even that would stop me. I would still run to her with my dress shoes filled with blood. My legs are starting to hurt already, but I push through. I'll run to her, I'll run until my legs give out and all the air is gone from my lungs. Then I'll fucking crawl to her if I have to. *I'm coming, moy slomannyy angel, just hang on.*

CHAPTER 22
No Soul to Sell

THAT SLICE TO my cheek hurt a hell of a lot more than I was expecting. I hate that Maison made Viktor hear me scream in pain when he did it. My cheek stings; Maison cut me deep, and the gash splits open even more when I move any part of my face. This drug needs to hurry up and wear off before he's done playing with me and decides to actually kill me.

"Well that was fun, I wonder how mad Viktor will be once I kill his little fuck toy. Poor guy will have to find a new redhead to have fun with." I ignore the horrible things he's saying to me; his words mean nothing to me. He means nothing. "How's your face feeling, sunshine?" he mocks.

"It's a good thing I never got you to do my torturing for me—you suck at it," I retort.

Maison kicks me in the ribs again, and this time, it sucks the air right out of my lungs. A rib cracks as his boot makes contact, and my abdomen is in excruciating pain. I can't take a breath without causing myself more pain.

"You just don't know when to stop running your mouth, do you? No wonder your mother hated you." The mention of my mother stings a little. "Speaking of Mommy, I went to pay her a visit. I knew you wouldn't care if she died, but you would if someone killed her. It would bother you not knowing who it was, so I went to her shithole apartment to kill her, but the bitch beat me to it. Oh well, I have more people I can kill. I'll start with finding out where your dad's hiding, kill him first. Then I'll make my way back to Marco, Dante, and of course, Viktor. Then once they're gone, I'll move on to their wives and even that little girl."

I grind my teeth, anger bubbling up inside me at the mention of him killing the ones I love. I won't let that happen. I can't. Maison moves to a bag on the ground, crouching down on his knees and taking out weapons from it. He sets the knife he used on my face down in front of me. I eye the blade as if it's taunting me.

While he's distracted, I try to move my hand; my fingers start moving. *Yes! Come on, body, don't fail me now, fight!* I open and close my hand, getting the blood to flow back into it. My hands are weak, but I can move one enough to try and grab the knife. Maison is whistling away to himself while he picks out which weapon to kill me with.

"Hmm, what to choose..." he mutters to himself.

I slowly grab the knife, trying to not make any sound, as I tuck it under me, out of sight. "Maison," I whisper.

"What? If you"re going to beg, you're about two years too late," he says.

I keep my voice low so it's hard for him to hear me, causing him to move closer to me. "You know the drug you gave me?"

"Yeah, what about it?" he asks, annoyed. I mumble something under my breath. "I can't fucking hear you! Speak up!" he yells, moving beside me.

"It wore off," I whisper.

"What? I don't have time for this shit; what the fuck are you saying?" he yells again, grabbing my face and lifting me slightly off the ground.

"I said fuck you!"

I plunge the knife right through his throat, his eyes widening as he chokes on his own blood. He hits the ground, letting go of me, and my body joins him on the cement driveway. I did it; they're safe. I start to feel lightheaded from the pain of my injuries. My name is being yelled in the distance before my eyes close, sucking me back into the darkness once again.

CHAPTER 23

With Love Comes Death

Viktor

I CONTINUE TO yell Violet's name up the driveway. She's laying in the middle of it, her hair fanning out around her like a halo. I fall to my knees beside her. My legs are numb, and I'm gasping for breath, sweat beading off my forehead. But I can't pay attention to my own pain right now. All I care about is focusing on the woman I love lying unconscious, covered in blood in front of me.

I lift her head, cradling it. "Violet," I call to her, but she's not responding, not even to my touch. I check her pulse; it's weak, but at least I know she's still breathing.

"Jesus fuck, V," Dante says beside me.

"What has he done to you, moy slomannyy angel?" I say to her, my heart breaking seeing her like this.

It must have been Maison; there's no sign of anyone else around, and his body is next to hers with a knife through his throat. I knew something wasn't right in that fucker's voice, and it was his laugh I heard after he made her scream.

I lift Violet up off the ground and carry her in my arms. Her body feels so much smaller and fragile at this moment, and my heart breaks even more. I'm trying to get hold of my own emotions so I can get her some help. As I'm about to carry her inside, Dante yells out.

"Is that motherfucker still alive?"

I stop, looking over my shoulder at Maison, who's crawling pathetically toward a bag on the ground. He's trailing a pool of blood behind him, but he's still very much alive. How? I have no fucking idea.

I turn to Marco, who's closest to me. "Take her inside, I'll be there in a minute," I tell him, passing Violet into his arms.

It's killing me to give her to him. I don't want anyone else to touch her, but I need to deal with Maison, and Marco will look after her. He leaves the rest of us to take her inside, and I'm now left standing with Dante and two of my men. I walk toward Maison, who's still crawling, and kick the bag away from him. Various weapons spill out of it onto the concrete, including a handgun. Well, I know why he was so desperate for the bag now.

I stare at Maison with disdain, circling him like a vulture. Rage consumes me, turning my vision to red. This piece of shit tried to take Violet away from me, tortured her and made me listen to her screams. I stand beside Maison's head and lift my right foot. I stomp it down on his head, over and over again, as hard as I can. I don't stop until his brains are turned to mush beneath my shoe. Satisfied, I slide my shoe across the pavement to get his blood and brains off it. I spit on Maison's body, then adjust my composure and head inside the cabin.

Marco has Violet laid out on a table. There's papers scattered all over the floor. I step on them as I walk toward Violet, not having a care in the world but her. There could be acid on the ground eating away at my shoes, and I still wouldn't pay any attention to it. Standing at the side of the table, I gently grab Violet's face, turning it over to examine her. She has a huge gash on her right cheek, the blood from the wound starting to crust around it. Other than that, though, there's no other head or facial injuries on her.

I move my hands down to her stomach, looking for stab wounds. She has blood all over her, and I'm not sure if it's hers or Maison's. I lift her shirt up, exposing her stomach and see red, angry bruising along her ribs. There's a shoe imprint in her skin, and I don't doubt she has a few broken ribs if he kicked her hard enough to leave an imprint. I wish I could kill that cocksucker all over again.

Gently, I touch the bruises on her skin. *Fuck, Violet.* It kills me, seeing these marks on her. I've never felt so helpless. I don't know how to fix this, fix her. I should've never let her go alone; her stubbornness will be the death of me.

"We need to get her to the hospital; did our men find another way here?" I ask Marco.

"Yes, they are close. Nico said five minutes."

I nod and look back at my beautiful broken angel. The next five minutes are going to feel like a fucking hour.

"I don't understand, how did Violet get so injured? She could kill Maison so easily. How did he get the upper hand?" Dante questions.

"Packhan! I found this on the ground outside," one of my men says, barging in the room, holding a syringe in his hand.

I take it from him, holding it up to show Dante and Marco. "There's your answer—he drugged her."

"Fuck," Dante curses. We all stop talking when we hear cars coming up the driveway.

"Our men are here," Marco announces.

I pick up Violet from the table and carry her out of the cabin, sprinting as fast as I can without dropping her. Marco opens the car door for me, and I climb in with Violet still in my arms. I sit with her legs across my lap and cradle her head to my chest, kissing the top of her head.

"Just hold on a little longer, moya lyubov. My love, just a little longer."

CHAPTER 24

A Savior Can Only Save So Many

Violet

I STRAIN MY eyes open against the bright lights. My body doesn't hurt as much as it did before I blacked out, and I try to open my eyes wider to see where I am. Beige walls fill my vision; I must be in a hospital. It reeks of antiseptic. I turn my head to the side and see Viktor sleeping in a chair beside my bed. He looks tired and stressed, even though he's sleeping. I lift my weak hand and place it on top of his.

He jolts awake. "Violet," he says excitedly.

"Hi," I say, giving him a small smile.

My voice is hoarse and dry, and I'm desperate for a drink of water. They must have flushed my body with something to remove what was left of the drug, giving me a dry mouth. Viktor grabs the hand I placed on his and kisses it.

"I almost lost you," he whispers, the pained look on his face hurting me more than my ribs.

"I'm here, you came for me," I reply, a little surprised that he did.

Viktor's forehead creases, and he looks even more hurt. "Of course I did, Violet, I—I love you." That final piece of ice entrapping my heart melts away at his confession. "I know you might not be in love with me, too, but that won't change my love for you," he explains.

Oh, how wrong he is. I do love him, I just haven't had the guts to say it. If I say it, then it makes it all too real, and if it's real, it can break. I guess it's going to break me either way once I tell him I'm leaving. While I was blacked out, alone with my darkness, I had time to think about a lot of things, and I realized this life isn't for me anymore.

"Viktor…"

"V! You're up!" Dante interrupts, walking into the room.

"How are you feeling?" Marco asks, coming in behind him.

"Hey, I'm okay, whatever the doctor gave me seems to be working."

"What the hell happened? Why did Maison do this?" Dante asks.

I put the conversation with Viktor on hold about me leaving and told them everything that happened.

"I never knew I was the cause of his mother's death. I'm sorry, Violet. If I had known he hated me so much, I never would have agreed to let him work for you," Marco says with remorse.

"It's not your fault, Marco. Even if you didn't accidentally get his mother killed, he would have tried to hurt me anyway. He seemed mainly pissed about the fact I friend-zoned him, so he was a loose cannon from the beginning. If he had this type of anger inside him, any of us could have set him off," I reassure him. "I'm just glad I got to kill him before he got to any of you."

"Well, actually, he was still alive when we found you. Barely, but still very much breathing," Dante says.

"What?" I shout.

"Viktor took care of it, though, squashed his brains right into the pavement," Dante says proudly.

I whip my head around to Viktor. "You did that?"

He nods. "I would have done more if he wasn't already so close to death," he says bitterly.

Viktor has killed for me before but never that gruesomely. I have never had a man love me, and now, I have a man who loves me and is willing to kill any man that hurts me—and I'm about to lose him.

A lump forms in my throat. "I need to have a moment alone with Viktor," I tell Marco and Dante.

"Sure," Marco says, leaving the room with Dante.

"What's wrong, my broken angel?" Viktor asks.

He's looking at me so adoringly. Fuck, this hurts. *Just do it, Violet, rip it off like a fucking Band-Aid covering the scars on my heart.*

I take a deep breath. "I'm leaving, Viktor."

I almost choke on my words, not wanting them to come out. That loving look in his eyes is still there, but now becoming clouded with sadness and confusion.

"What? What do you mean you're leaving?" he asks.

"While I was knocked out, I thought a lot about us, about you and my life. I realized that I need a break from this life. I've lost myself over the years, and I don't know how to get back to the woman I once was. I'm grateful for the girls I have saved, but everyone's right; I can't save them all, and it's going to keep taking more and more pieces of me if I keep trying. So I'm leaving. I don't know for how long. I want you to come with me, but I know you can't. You have responsibilities here, Viktor, I can't ask you to leave the Bratva for me; it means everything to you."

It's hard to breathe. Tears threaten to flow, but I hold them back. I gaze into Viktor's eyes, seeing the hurt my words have caused him staring back at me.

"You're right, I can't leave," he confirms, sounding defeated.

I nod in agreement, trying desperately not to cry. Of course the first man I fall in love with in years loves me back, and I can't be with him. The fates have always played cruel jokes on me, but this is the cruelest joke they have ever played. I'm choosing myself for once, and it's one of the hardest things I've ever done. I feel like I'm throwing away a chance for us to be together, but I need to do this. As much as it hurts, it has to happen.

"If this is what you want, then I can't stop you. I won't be the man that makes you change what you want in life just for me." Viktor stands. "Goodbye, Violet," he says quietly, bending down to kiss my forehead.

His lips linger there for a few seconds, and I soak up the feeling of his lips touching my skin for the last time. When he pulls away, I want to beg him to put them back. Viktor doesn't look at me, just turns his back and heads for the door. I know he's hurting, but I wish he wasn't walking away so easily. I need to tell him how I truly feel; I can't just let him leave without knowing the truth.

"Viktor." He stops in his tracks when I call his name. "I love you, too."

His shoulders tense, but he doesn't turn around. Just when I think he might look at me one last time, he starts walking straight ahead. The door shuts behind him, and I break. The tears I've been holding back stream from my eyes, leaving salty stains in their wake. I sit there in the hospital bed alone, surrounded by my own sorrow.

MARCO, DANTE AND I are back at the penthouse after the doctor discharged me and told me to just take my meds and get plenty of rest the next few weeks. There's nothing else they can do for broken ribs; they'll have to heal on their own, so I'm stuck with taking pain meds for a while.

I'm sitting on the rooftop overhang like I always do when I need to think. It hurt like a bitch getting up here, but it was worth it for the beautiful view of the city. Up here, New York City seems so peaceful. From up here, the evil that lurks in this city is covered by tall buildings and bright lights. I'm going to miss killing men in this city.

"I figured you would be up here," Dante yells from down below, climbing up the wall ladder I used to get up here.

He sits down beside me, joining me in watching the city. After Viktor left my hospital room, Marco and Dante came in shortly afterward, finding me a blubbering mess. Dante has never seen me cry before, and Marco only has once; the night we first met. They were both shocked and looked like they wanted to kill Viktor because they thought he did something. Once I told them why I was so upset, and that I was leaving, they had just as bad of a reaction as Viktor did.

"Damn, the city does look a hell of a lot better from up here. I should come up here more often," Dante says.

"Well, you can claim this spot as your own once I leave. I'll be nice and let you have it," I say sarcastically.

Dante smirks. "Are you sure you wanna do this, V?" he asks.

"Dante, I need to. As much as I enjoy killing men—"

He cuts me off. "No, I'm not talking about that. I meant with Viktor. Are you sure you wanna leave him?"

"Of course I don't. I don't want to leave any of you. But with Viktor, I can't be the woman he needs. I have things I need to work on. I need to start fixing myself, and loving myself first. I made the right decision saying goodbye to him." *At least I think I did.*

"Well, if you think this is the right decision, then I can't convince you otherwise," he states. "I just... I'm gonna miss you, Red."

"Dante, you're acting like I'm leaving forever. I'll come visit you guys in Italy still, just maybe not as often as I normally would," I clarify.

"You better. I don't wanna have to hunt you down for making Lily cry because she can't see her Aunt Violet," he says, cross with the idea. "You know when my little girl cries, I would do just about anything to make her stop. I'm a tough man, but not with her."

I laugh. "I won't disappoint her. I'll visit. I promise." And when it comes to Lily, I always keep my promises.

"Madonna, how the hell did you two get up there?" Marco shouts at us. We both look down at him.

"Ah, maybe the giant ladder over there; put your glasses on, old man!" Dante yells back at him.

"Fuck you, Stronzo! I'll come up there and throw you off, then we'll see who the old man is."

I shake my head at them fighting; ah, brotherly love. Marco climbs the ladder to join us.

"Are you two aware this is a perfect view for a sniper to kill us?" Marco points out.

I roll my eyes at him. "How about you stop thinking about death for a few minutes and just enjoy it," I tell him.

"Fine, you're right," Marco says, lifting his hands up in mock surrender. He sits down on the other side of me. "So, what happens now? Have you figured out where you're gonna go?" he asks.

"I have a few places in mind. I spoke to Natalia. She will be running the Help Line, and I told her if you need help with anything, you can reach out to her. She's good. I trust her to take care of things," I say.

He nods. "I'm not worried; you trained her well. I know she can handle the job. It's you I'm worried about. Are you going to be able to let this all go and let her do things instead of you?"

I sigh. "I am, actually. I think deep down, this was always my plan. I just got so lost in wanting to save more women, and the satisfaction I got from killing the men that hurt them.. Then, when Maison tried to kill me, I realized I needed to do this now for myself before it's too late. I never was afraid of dying, and I'm still not. But I *am* afraid of dying and having the only things I've done in life be for other people. I love you guys, and working for you, Marco, was the best decision I ever made. I have a real family now, and

I saved women, which is amazing. Please don't take this as me throwing that away," I explain.

"I don't think that. I know how grateful you are, and we're both grateful we got a sister. Sorry, let me rephrase that; we have a sister," he corrects, giving me a hug.

"Alright, enough. Or someone's gonna start crying, and it might be me," Dante says.

"Figo," Marco calls Dante.

Dante feigns offense, gasping and putting a hand on his chest. "I'm telling Sabrina you called me a pussy for finally expressing my feelings," he teases.

"Don't you fucking dare! I'll never hear the end of it, then she will make me talk about mine!" Marco complains.

I laugh. "I'm gonna miss this."

I link arms with both of them as we watch the sunset go down. Tomorrow, I start a new life again; a life just for me.

CHAPTER 25

Sacrifices

Viktor
Four Months Later

I SIT IN my office at the club, like I do every night. Each night, I keep thinking the more time I spend here focusing on work, the less I'll think of Violet. I'm a fool for thinking work could ever ease my mind of her. I don't want to forget about her; I want her now and always. Violet was on my mind nearly every day when she was here, and it's gotten worse since she left. I miss everything about that woman—her taste, her smell, the little smirk she makes when she's trying not to smile. I even miss her sassy nature.

There's nothing I wouldn't give just to hear her sarcastic comments, or have her try to fight with me just to watch her submit to me later. But most of all, I miss her warmth. Even when Violet was being cold, she still had this infectious warmth to her. Now, it's gone, and my life feels colder than it did before I met her.

There's a light knock on my door, and Dimitry walks in. He sighs, looking at me behind my desk.

"Chto?"

"What?" I ask.

"Okay, I know you are the boss, but as your family, I say this with love: what the fuck are you doing, brother?" Dimitry asks.

"What do you mean? I am working," I tell him.

"No, you are moping, and you have been like this since that Violet woman left."

"My woman," I correct him. Even if she isn't physically here, she will always be mine to me.

"Well, if she is your woman, then why aren't you with her?" he questions.

"I've told you why, brother," I reply, getting annoyed with him.

"You have been like this for four months now; either do something about it, or move on," he stresses.

"I can't seem to do either of those things. I don't want any other woman, but I can't be with her while still being the head of this Bratva, so moping is my only option," I snap.

"If this woman really means that much to you, then you should retire early. I'm not trying to take your place or your legacy away from you. You have done your father proud over the years with the things you've done. No one would blame you for retiring early; the men will understand," he says.

"I don't know if I'm ready to give all this up," I admit to him. "The Bratva is my blood. It's all I know, and my father would be rolling in his grave if I gave all that up for love."

"Okay, then are you ready to give her up?"

"I already have, I didn't stop her from leaving," I say with regret.

"I'm not talking about letting her move away, I'm talking about giving her up completely in your heart. Think about it, brother; which one hurts losing the most? The Bratva or Violet?"

Hearing her name sparks a pain in my chest. "Enough, you've been listening to your marriage counselor a little too much," I snap at him.

"Maybe, but she speaks the truth. Think about it, Viktor, and whatever decision you make, I will stand by you."

I nod as he leaves the room. He probably thinks I don't want to retire because I don't trust him to run things, but that's not it. I know Dimitry would do just as well as I have, and my men respect him—so did my father. We are the same when it comes to running the Bratva.

And then there's Mama; I can't just leave her. Run off and start a new life. I would still need to see her at least once a week, or have her move in. How would I even make that work? I think further about what Dimitry said: losing Violet forever is hurting me more than the thought of giving up the Bratva. But I'm worried that if I give everything up for her, and she doesn't feel the same about me as she once did, what will I do? Maybe that's a risk I'm willing to take just to see her again.

I think deep down in my gut I have already made my decision. I've been sitting in my office every night trying to think of ways to get her back, of rearranging my life so it would work for us. Now all that's left to do is find her. *I am coming for you, moy slomannyy angel, for the last time.*

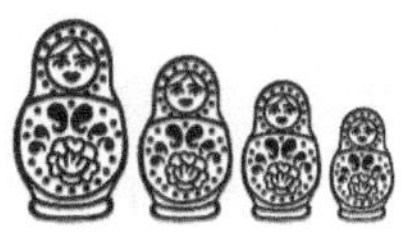

I'VE BEEN STRONG the past few months, not asking Marco where Violet ran off to. So when I finally asked him after four months, he must have taken pity on me, because he had no problem telling me where she was. All he asked was that I promise to take care of her, and that if she doesn't want me there, to leave and not put up a fight. I, of course, agreed, but that won't be happening. I can't lose her again.

Marco said she moved to a little town in Sudbury, Massachusetts. He mentioned she picked that location because it was a nice, quiet, small town, and she wouldn't be too far away from New York so she could still visit. I was expecting her to move to a whole other country, but I'm glad she stayed close by. Makes me showing up there a whole lot easier.

Before I left, I spoke with Mama and told her I was going after Violet. I promised to still cook with her once a week, even if we are just talking on the phone while doing it, that I would find a way to make it work. She didn't seem to mind; she was more happy for me that I finally found a woman I love and want to be with. I told her she could even move here. She might like the small town better than New York.

I arrive in Sudbury, Massachusetts, and this town is definitely a change from New York. Small, family-owned shops fill the streets and with friendly, smiling shop owners; yeah, a hell of a lot different than New York. I must look insane to these people. I'm casually dressed in jeans and a black T-shirt, but my muscular build and the scars on my face don't exactly fit into the warm, fuzzy town feel.

I wonder if Violet felt that way her first time coming here. Marco didn't know what area or street she was living in. Violet probably wanted to keep things as secret as possible so people like me didn't show up. This is a small town, though, and I'm sure if I ask someone around here, they will tell me exactly where she is. People like to gossip in small towns, especially when outsiders move in.

There's a convenience store across the street from where I'm standing. I'll start there. I cross the street and make my way to the shop. The door chimes when I open it and walk in.

"Hello there, big fella, welcome to Mindy's Convenience. You must be just passing through; are you a truck driver?" she asks, all smiles.

A truck driver? Is that what I look like to these people? I guess it's better than them thinking I'm an escaped convict—or an ex-Bratva boss.

"No, actually, I was wondering if you can help me. I'm trying to track down an old... friend. She just moved here, and we lost touch. Her name is Violet."

"No, no one by the name of Violet in this town, only the flowers down at Christy's flower shop." The lady tries to joke with me.

I plaster a fake smile on my face. "Right, well maybe if I describe her, that might help. She's short, about 5 '1, has beautiful red hair, and—"

Before I can continue, the woman cuts me off, recognition plastered on her face. "Oh, you mean Stephanie! She's a wonderful girl; she just moved into the house on Conquerall Bank a few months ago. It's about fifteen minutes out of town. She bought the Miller's old house. It's a little small for my liking, and a bit dark, too."

I didn't ask, I think to myself. I thank the woman and leave the shop. Violet changed her name to Stephanie. It's not a bad name, just doesn't suit her.

I walk back down to my rental car. I couldn't drive my hellcat here; it would draw more attention to me than my appearance already has, so I left it with Dimitry. As I walk toward the car, I pass by a light post with a Missing Persons ad taped to it. It catches my eye, and I stop to read it. A man named Glen went missing a few weeks ago. It says he runs the town's farmers' markets. Hmm, interesting, seems strange a man like him would go missing in a town like this.

I get in the car, paying no more attention to the missing man. My nerves are starting to get to me. I'm not a man who gets nervous, but I haven't seen Violet in four months. What if her feelings have changed? She said she loved me once, but maybe this time apart has made her realize she doesn't. I try not to think too negatively about that and head to her house.

I arrive at Violet's exactly ten minutes later. The convenience store woman said it was fifteen, but I'm a man on a mission and don't have time to waste. I just need to see her, even if her feelings have changed, just seeing her again is enough for me.

The house is small, but nice. It fits Violet well; she has painted it black, but has planted brightly coloured flowers around it. Making it look like darkness surrounded by light—much like my Violet.

I walk up the driveway to the front steps when I stop short on the first one, hearing something. I try to listen closely; there's a scraping sound coming from the backyard as if someone is clawing at something. I head toward the backyard quietly, and that's when I see her. Violet is hunched over, working on her garden. She's wearing black leggings, and a ratty, old white T-shirt, with her hair done up in a messy bun on top of her head.

The sun shines down on her red hair, making it look lighter. Her back is to me as she's clawing at the earth with her gardening tool. I'm mesmerized by her now, like I was the first time, and even with dirt on her shirt, covered in plant debris, she still takes my breath away. I would throw her right in that dirt and fuck her right now if I could. Maybe later.

I get closer to her as she stands, admiring her work. Now standing right behind her, Violet must have finally heard me, because she whips around, ready to stab me with her clawing tool.

I catch her wrist, stopping her. "Hello, moy slomannyy angel, it's only been four months since you've stopped working, and you're already getting rusty," I tease.

Her eyes widen, surprised to see me here. "Viktor!" she shouts, throwing her arms around my neck and hugging me. There it is; that warmth I've been missing. I wrap my arms around her tightly, afraid she will slip away from me again. How could I have ever thought I could live without her? Having her in my arms again is the only sign I need to know I made the right choice in leaving the Bratva.

Violet

I CAN'T BELIEVE Viktor's here. He's really here. I haven't stopped thinking about him since the day I left New York to start a new life. The first day I moved here, all I kept thinking about was how nice this place would be to share with Viktor. I almost cracked right there and called him, begging him to come see me even for just a day. *Am I dreaming?* I remove my head from his chest and crane my neck to look up at him, our arms still around each other.

"What are you doing here? Did Marco tell you where I was?" I ask.

"Yes, I haven't bothered him since you left, but I needed to see you, so he told me where you were, but I had to ask a shop owner for the address. She didn't really seem keen with the house you bought," he says.

"Oh, yup, that would be Ms. Anderson. For a cheerful broad, she's a bit judgmental." I laugh. "Why did you come, Viktor? I mean I'm happy to see you, but I don't understand... You told me you couldn't leave the Bratva, so are you just here to visit?" I ask him, hoping it's more than just that. His tender gaze makes my heart burn; not with pain, but with happiness and warmth.

"No, malyshka, I didn't come here just to visit. Seeing your face again, I don't think I could walk away from you even if I tried, or even if you did stab me with your gardening tool," he jokes, and I smirk, glancing over at the tool on the ground. Viktor places his hand on my chin, guiding my attention back to him. "I decided to retire early, Violet. I left the Bratva," he states.

I stare at him, shocked. "What?"

"The Bratva and my family were the two most important things in my life. Then you came along, with your hellfire, and then I had three things that were most important to me. But then you left, and I realized I could live without the Bratva, but not you. I don't just want you anymore, Violet... I need you. Dimitry can run the Bratva fine without me, my men will be fine without me. I'm not fine without you."

My heart pulses rapidly at him confessing his emotions to me. He chose me. He left the Bratva for me, because he loves me. He really loves me. It's hard to believe when you've never had someone choose you before; my instincts from my past traumas are telling me it's all bullshit. That he couldn't have possibly done all that for me, but he did. The truth in his eyes is bright and clear, and the love he feels for me. It brings a tear to my eye. My eyes begin to water, and a single tear falls down my cheek. Viktor swipes at it with his thumb, hurt and realization forming on his face.

"If your feelings have changed for me, I understand," he says, sounding wounded. He thinks I'm crying because I don't want him anymore.

I give him an annoyed look. "Viktor, I didn't leave because I didn't want to be with you. I left because I needed to, and I was afraid if I didn't get my own darkness under control that I would stay that same cold-hearted bitch forever. You give me shelter from myself, you quiet my darkness. But I needed to learn how to quiet it myself, because I didn't want to rely on you for that, and you end up resenting me for it. But we have a problem, Viktor. Actually, we have a lot of problems, but one we share. I have been working on myself a lot these past few months—gardening, doing things that I've always wanted to do but just never had the time for, and I'm happy here. Way happier than I ever was in New York, but every time I do something I enjoy, I keep thinking about how much I would rather be enjoying myself here with you. See, I can live without you, Viktor, I just don't want to."

His look softens once he realizes where I'm going with this.

"I'm not going to be an easy woman to be with, Viktor, you know that. That being said, I do want to try to make us work," I say, waiting for his rejection.

But it never comes. Instead, Viktor grabs my face with both hands and kisses me with such love and passion, a bullet could shoot right through my head, and I would die happy just being loved by this man.

Viktor breaks our kiss. "Ty ne predstavlyayesh', kakoy schastlivoy ty menya sdelal, moy angel." *You have no idea how happy you made me, my angel.*

There he goes with the Russian again. "English, Viktor," I snap.

He smirks at me. "Net, learn Russian if you want to know the sweet things I say to you," he teases.

I slap his chest playfully, the word "Russian" jogging a thought in my mind. "You mentioned Dimitry is the new Pakhan, but what about your club?" I ask, concerned. Viktor loves that club, and it's a big money maker for him.

"Dimitry can run it; it's just a club, Violet, but if you want to, we can always visit. We can even use my old office for old times' sake," he says with a wink.

The corner of my mouth lifts slightly at his cheeky pass. "We can definitely visit. I would love to meet your cousin and your mom," I say, hopeful that he actually wants me to meet her.

"Good, because you're meeting them whether you like it or not," he replies, his dominant aura returning.

"Are you sure I'm not too much trouble for her?" I joke.

"No, malyshka, she can handle you, but speaking of trouble, I saw this Missing Persons ad for that Glen man," he says, eyeing me suspiciously. "You wouldn't happen to know anything about that, would you?"

I put a hand on my chest, pretending to be shocked. "Are you assuming I had something to do with his disappearance? If so, then you would be right. He was always checking out underaged girls at the market. He was creepy, and I couldn't let his nasty, perverted intentions infect this sweet town, so I took care of him. But in my defense, I killed him because I wanted to, not because someone asked me to, or needed my help, so it doesn't count."

Viktor smirks. "Whatever you say, my little killer, I'll just have to keep a better eye on you and make sure you don't get into any more trouble."

"And what if I do?" I tantalize him. Viktor swiftly throws me over his shoulder. "Ah, Viktor!" I laugh.

"Don't tease me, Violet, it's been too long since I've had you, and I plan on making up for lost time. You won't be leaving this house for the next few weeks."

He slaps my ass as he carries me over his shoulder, up the stairs and into our new home. And our new life of darkness, together.

EPILOGUE

Two Years Later
Violet

VIKTOR AND I are cuddling on the couch, getting ready to pick a movie to watch. It's become our nightly routine. These past two years here with Viktor have been nothing but pure bliss. It's taken some getting used to, going from living a life of crime and chaos, to peace and, well, a little boredom at times, but we make the most of it.

We are still not like any traditional couple. Most couples have greenhouses and family game rooms, whereas Viktor built a weapons shed in the backyard, so I can still practice my knife throwing, and he can make sure we are ready in case any of our enemies from the past decide to show up. I love the life we have built, and our relationship has only gotten stronger over the years, but Viktor has been acting a little strange lately. Usually, I'm very good at reading him and can tell he's been hiding something from me.

"So moya lyubov, which one are you feeling tonight, horror or thriller?" he asks.

"Mm, I'm feeling more thriller this time," I say.

"Thriller it is, then; you pick one, and I'll go make us some popcorn."

He gives me a quick peck on the forehead, then leaves the room. I scroll through the list of movies, looking for one that interests me, when suddenly the TV screen goes black. Not just the screen—the whole house. Either there's a town power outage, or someone cut our fucking power. I call out for Viktor, but he doesn't respond. *Shit.* I feel around, searching for my phone on the couch, my eyes not adjusting to the darkness yet. My phone lights up, wedged between the cushions. I pull it out and turn it over, Viktor's name flashing on the screen. *Where is he? Why is he calling me?*

"Viktor, where are you?" I ask, worried.

"Don't panic, malyshka, I am outside. It was me who cut the power," he admits.

"Why?" I ask, confused.

"Stop asking questions and listen to me carefully, Violet." All my confusion leaves my body and is replaced by heated butterflies in my stomach when his voice turns husky and demanding. "We have been watching so many thriller movies lately, I thought it would be fun to create one of our own. You're going to go hide, and when I find you, I get to do whatever the fuck I want to you," he growls. My pussy instantly gets wet at his threat, and the idea of me hiding and him finding me just so he can ravish me in the end. "You have ten seconds, Violet, starting now!"

I drop my phone and bolt to the front hall closet at the end of the house. My heart is bounding with adrenaline as I get to it, throwing the door open. There's not really a lot of places to hide in this house since it's only a bungalow. So the closet, even though it's a typical place for someone to hide, is my best bet. There's enough stuff in here that I can pile some of it on top of me to hide myself better.

My eyes have finally adjusted to the darkness, and the silhouette of our suitcases are in front of me. I push them aside so I can squeeze my body in behind them. Once I get in, I move further back into the closet and lay on the floor, pushing the two suitcases in front of me, blocking me from sight. I pull at a jacket sleeve hanging down in front of me, pulling it off the hanger and draping it over me, shielding me even more.

My heart's racing in anticipation. I try to control my breathing, but it's hard after running as fast as I did, and it's hot as fuck in this closet. Viktor's footsteps are nearing, getting closer to the closet with each step he takes. There's a faint shadow of his feet between the cracks of the two suitcases, and his footsteps stop. His boots squeak along the floor as he turns in front of the closet. Viktor slowly opens the door, and I put a hand over my mouth to cover my breathing. I lay there quietly, not moving a muscle as I listen for his next move.

I must have hid a hell of a lot better than I thought, because the next sound I hear is Viktor's footsteps retreating back in the other direction. I release a breath in relief. He left the closet door open, so maybe I can sneak out and hide somewhere else. Just when I think I have fooled him, a hand wraps around my ankle, and I'm pulled forcefully out of the closet. My body slides across the floor, and I scream as Viktor drags me to the living room. I kick at him, trying to fight him off even though my arousal is practically dripping down my fucking legs.

Viktor drops my ankle and straddles my hips, caging me in. "Found you, moy slomannyy angel," he growls menacingly.

Only the outline of his face and body are visible, but I don't need to see him to feel the sheer dominance and power he's giving off. My body tingles in excitement and a little bit of fear for all the things he plans to do to me. I slap at his chest, not wanting to give into him so easily. "You can fight all you want, Violet, but I found you. And I'm collecting my prize."

Viktor flips me over and roughly pulls my sleep shorts down and off my legs. I don't wear panties around the house, because Viktor just rips them off me, so I gave up wearing them. He slaps my ass hard and runs his tongue along my lower spine.

"Fuck, I can't wait to be inside you; I missed your pussy," he rasps.

"You just had it this morning," I scoff.

"That was eight hours ago, too long." I moan as he spreads my ass cheeks apart. "You didn't hide very well, Violet, I expected better from you," he says.

"Maybe I wanted you to find me," I breathe.

"Mhm, I think you did, moya gryaznaya devchonka." *My dirty girl.*

Viktor circles my entrance with the head of his cock before thrusting it deep inside me. I cry out from the sudden roughness and his thick cock stretching me open. He sucks in a breath through his teeth.

"Fuck, I never get tired of how good you feel," he groans.

Viktor starts fucking me hard from behind, and I claw at the ground, needing something to grip. Surprise jolts through me as his thumb—coated in my arousal—grazes my asshole. Viktor has never touched me there before. We haven't explored anal play, and I'm a little nervous to start. I try and move his hand away, but he grabs both my wrists and pins them behind my back.

"If you want me to stop, use your safe word, but if not, don't try and stop me from giving you pleasure," he growls at me, like I've offended him for even daring to stop him.

I trust Viktor and have never needed to use my safe word with him, and I don't plan to start now. I push down my worries and let him continue. Viktor slowly and gently pushes his thumb inside. It's uncomfortable at first, but once my body relaxes, I'm not ashamed to say it feels really fucking good. I moan as he slowly moves his thumb in and out,, the same time as his cock thrusts in and out of my pussy.

"I'll be taking your ass soon, Violet. Not tonight, but I want to claim all your holes as mine."

I moan louder at the idea of having him claim my ass just as much as he's claimed the rest of my body. Viktor's thrusts get faster; he always fucks me like he can never get enough. Like being inside me just isn't enough for him. He lets go of my wrists with his other hand and brings it to my throat, lifting my head up. My back arches, and my ass presses against his abdomen. He's plunging deeper at this angle, and I cry out when he hits my G-spot. Viktor slides two fingers up my neck and past my chin toward my mouth. I open for him, then close my lips around his fingers, sucking on them as if they were his cock.

"Do you like having all your holes filled, malyshka?" he asks.

I nod, getting lost in the sensation of being so filled by him. Viktor pulls his fingers out of my mouth and my ass. I don't even have time to whine at the loss of them, because he flips me over so fast, I get light-headed. He throws my legs over his shoulders and fucks into me harder then he was before. I slide my hand down to my pussy and rub my clit, massaging it while he fucks me.

"Make yourself come on my cock, Violet, then I'll give you your surprise."

I don't even register what he said, too focused on my increasing pleasure. My body tingles, and I clench my pussy around Viktor's cock, coming all over it. Lost in my orgasm, Viktor slides something onto my ring finger. I look down at my hand in the dark, something shiny glinting in the darkness. He's still fucking me, but his thrusts have slowed as I stare at my hand, and the engagement ring he just placed on it.

"I thought asking you to marry me while my cock was buried deep inside you was the best way to do it," he admits. I'm still staring at my hand in shock, lost for words. "Will you marry me, moy lyubov?" he asks. "And if you think I will stop fucking you if you say no, you're wrong. I will continue to fuck you and make you come until you say yes," he threatens.

"You didn't even need to ask me, Viktor. Yes, I'll marry you," I moan, and his thrusts pick up speed. He drops my legs from his shoulders and bends down to kiss me. We stay on the living room floor, fucking like animals. "I love you, Viktor."

"I love you, too, Violet."

ACKNOWLEDGMENTS & WHAT'S TO COME

Thank you so much for reading Violet and Viktor's story. I hope you enjoyed reading about these two, and their chaotic Dark Love story. I have been wanting to write their story for years now, and I'm so happy to have finally shared it with you all. If you enjoyed reading about the Berlusconi crime family, and want to hear more about how Dante and Marco met their wives, then stay tuned. Exciting things are coming! I started with Violet and Viktor's story first in the series, because at the time, their story spoke to me on a deeper level. I was going through a breakup, and at times felt like Violet did toward love and relationships. There will be four books total in the Forms of Darkness series, and we will be going back in time to the beginning, before Violet found Viktor, and the Berlusconi men found their wives. Marco and Sabrina's story will be next, followed by Dante and Nikki's. Then, a secret someone's love story for the fourth and final book. The rest of the books in the series get much darker, the men are more morally grey, and the spicy scenes are spicier. So be prepared! Finally, thank you to my friends and family that have been so supportive through my writing journey and have stuck by me cheering me on, even when I felt like giving up.

ABOUT THE AUTHOR

J. Anne Scott

From the moment she could hold a crayon, J. Anne Scott was already creating worlds with her imagination. She painted, constructed sketches, and art became a kaleidoscopic realm of possibilities for her creativity to roam freely. A true romantic at heart, as an adult, she found herself drawn to the world of passion and longing, captivated by romance novels under the covers long after bedtime. Erotica, with all its intimacy and raw emotion, called to her like a hidden mystery between each new page.

Now, after years of reading, dreaming, and daring, this Nova Scotia-based author has transformed the secrets and desires of her inner world into her very first publication. Her debut novel is not just a cookie-cutter romance story; it is a breath held too long, waiting to be set free, a brushstroke of pulsating desire across the canvas of longing, and a love letter to every reader who's ever yearned for more than just a typical "happy ending."

Written by my sister, Megan June, the poet.

www.ingramcontent.com/pod-product-compliance
Lightning Source LLC
Chambersburg PA
CBHW032013050726
47590CB00006B/2158